The patterns on Foundry Editions' covers have been designed to capture the visual heritage of the Mediterranean. This one is inspired by the architecture of the AAU Anastas Studio in Bethlehem. It was created by Hélène Marchal.

Palestinian author KARIM KATTAN was born in 1989 in Jerusalem, grew up in Bethlehem, and holds a doctorate in comparative literature. His 2017 short-story collection *Préliminaires pour un verger futur* was a finalist for the Prix Boccace. *The Palace on the Higher Hill*, his first novel, won the 2021 Prix des Cinq Continents de la Francophonie, and his most recent novel, *Eden at Dawn*, was shortlisted for the 2024 Prix Renaudot.

JEFFREY ZUCKERMAN is a translator from French of numerous writers, including Jean Genet, Hervé Guibert, and Ananda Devi. In addition to the many awards and honours he has received for his work, he was named a Chevalier de l'ordre des Arts et des Lettres by the French government.

Cet ouvrage a bénéficié du soutien du Programme d'aide à la publication de l'Institut français.

THE PALACE
ON THE HIGHER HILL

KARIM KATTAN

The Palace
on the Higher Hill

Translation by Jeffrey Zuckerman

**FOUNDRY
EDITIONS**

I didn't know the driver. He didn't talk to me, didn't ask questions. I was alone in the back seat. Not even my aunt Jeannette was coming with me to the airport. They were glad to be rid of me. Even though I hadn't done anything. I turned and looked back at the valley in ashes and the two hills as they grew less distinct, along with the village, and Old Jihad's restaurant, it hurt, and the houses, our house and what was left of Joséphine's, and what was left of her flowers, it hurt, the village was empty, like it'd been abandoned or left to die, even though nothing had happened, nothing, the place looked like it'd been empty forever, had they all fled, the car rounded a corner, and everything was gone, even though nothing had happened, nothing, and I hadn't done a thing, what things I'd done I'd just imagined, and nothing had happened, just two gold-hued eyes in the night and soldiers climbing our hill in the drizzle, and now the village and the two hills and our house up there and Joséphine's further down, all now at the mercy of the wind, I turned to look straight ahead again because it hurt and suddenly there was the sea, suddenly blue, then, for the first time in my life, an airport, a plane.

Off to boarding school for me. Although I hadn't done a thing. Two weeks later a letter informed me my aunt Jeannette had died. Served her right.

7

There's something I have to confess to you. I hope you'll hear me out, after everything that's happened. I won't go so far as to ask you to accept what I've done, much less support it – all I ask is that you hear me out. I have to confess to you.

I killed a man. A settler. A man but a settler. A settler but a man. It sounds kind of bad, doesn't it, when I say it like that – but nothing could be further from the truth. You have to understand: he materialised before me, under the almond trees. He was already dead, like a ghost, so that didn't change a thing at all. Immaculate daylight dappled the almond trees' shadows. He didn't see Nawal, but she was the one guiding my hand. I had a gun. I'd come out of the house and sat down in the clearing. I'd found the revolver in Nawal and Ibrahim's bedroom. I'd come outside with a glass of lemonade in my hand and the gun in my pocket and these plans to put an end to my life in a bucolic, unremarkable place. How nice the weather can be when death blossoms, I was thinking. But the settler appeared out of nowhere. I shot him – well, more precisely, Nawal took my hand and shot him. She was tired, too. She was like a time-worn statue of a goddess. How pointless. I mean, a gun! If I hadn't fired the shot, he probably would have. That's what I think. But that doesn't change a thing. That's not an admission. Yes, I've come out and said that I killed a man yesterday, just like that, boom. Nothing more to it.

What I have to confess to you is different. The man, that settler (I haven't moved him, he's still there, under the almond trees, that doesn't change a thing, do you think his body's already beginning to rot?), was ugly. I know, I know, but he really was. Maybe I wouldn't have killed him if he'd been handsome enough. I probably wouldn't have. I might have let him kill me, and quivered with pleasure. If he'd been handsome enough to take away even Nawal's breath, if he'd been handsome enough to charm a demon, who knows, things might have gone differently. I might have straight-up asked him to kill me not with a gun but with those beautiful hands of his around my neck and I would have died with an orgasmic moan, with drool running down my chin.

Before he turned up, before I found the gun, before I decided to come outside to die under the almond trees, Nawal was whispering nasty things in my ears: "Go on, get out, go and face them, if just one of them falls when you shoot then that's a bird in the hand, go, don't be scared, I'll go first, they won't dare shoot me, I'll pump them full of fear, let's go now, I'm going first."

I was tired and I didn't want to expend even more energy; I wanted to die. The settler appeared before me and ended up saving me. So I've decided to talk to you, to confess everything to you. I don't have anyone left to talk to and I know, in spite of it all, in spite of the shudder I feel at the thought of writing to you, that you'll hear me out. That at first you'll feel the urge to delete this message. And I also know, because I do remember this much about you even at this point, I also know that you won't. You'll let out a weary sigh, and then you'll read on.

All this time that I've been locked up with Nawal, a whole equinox, three seasons, two months, I've needed to talk to someone because that way I can clear up any misunderstandings.

Well, lend me your ears, if you will.

It's the story of a beginning, I'd say. Or the story of an end.

I was born under a Bedouin moon. No idea what that means. Tante Jeannette always told me that, her tone implying a condition I had contracted and might well pass on to her.

She said that the day I was born, she came out of the house and got lost in the woods. She happened upon a beast with its guts ripped out. "An animal," she said, "a wahsh, a wild creature, all alone."

I always asked, "What kind of creature?"

"A creature, just some creature." And that creature – imagine whatever you like, a deer, a ghoul, a jackal, a mutant – already beginning to rot, started talking to my aunt, Tante Jeannette.

What it said I couldn't possibly guess.

Actually, whenever she told me the story, she would squint at me accusingly. Except she looked exactly like one of those raccoons in my comic books, so I'd always burst out laughing and she would turn and remark, "There you have it."

Here I am talking to you as if I didn't know you! "I was born" this and "my aunt Jeannette" that and so on and on. Nawal's done me in. The smoke's covered the horizon in the distance. The stone villages dotting the hills disappear at times behind the scrim of smoke like in a game of hide-and-seek. I can kind of tell that most of the buildings are just rubble now.

"The Bedouin moon." That was another one of Joséphine's expressions. Sometimes she talked about it when I was at her house, she'd look at the sky and cry out, "Well, that's a beautiful Bedouin moon if I ever saw one!" So, ever since I was little, all moons have been Bedouin. Which stirs up images in my mind, one way or another, of caravan moons, indomitable moons, racing across the desert toward oases of stars. A moon foreign to itself, not unlike this self in me that isn't me. Here we are, myself and this other self in me, in the garden behind this house overlooking Joséphine's garden and, in the moonlight, these two gardens haven't lost any of their shine.

Lately, scraps of us, you and me living together, have been resurfacing. I'm getting better at recalling who I was for those ten years with you. Much of it is still hazy and if that life has been wiped from my mind, just know it wasn't for lack of trying to hang on to it. Just this morning, I remembered that you wanted children. Memories came back of you leaving out brochures of children with huge smiles, catalogues to pick them from: handsome and well groomed, impish but well mannered, silly yet well behaved. There was even a range of colours to choose from: more sickly olive like me or glowing sprite like you? You wanted kids, and I wouldn't listen. As if, the second you brought up the topic, a dull din rose up around me and pulled me away. I remembered that this morning, as they were starting to encircle the village.

I never could have explained to you my awareness that I was born to witness the extinction of my people. But you – in all your attentiveness, all your sweetness – you were keen on children and prepared to wait until the end of eternity for me to agree.

Believe me, George, it wasn't my plan. It wasn't my plan to disappear from your life like this. It wasn't my plan to, I swear it, it wasn't my plan to wake up that day in a daze as the sun struggled to rise, it wasn't my plan to grope around on the nightstand for my phone, to tap at it and pick an airline, a departure time, an extra checked bag, without any real thought, of course I'd need two suitcases for a big trip, it wasn't my plan to not tell you, to slip away in the early-morning haze. It wasn't really my plan, forty-eight hours later, to reach the house, to strain to push this door open, to stagger into this drawing room. It wasn't my plan to, you might not believe me, that's on you, it wasn't my plan to not write to you all this time. Not a single text, not a call, not an email, not even an old-fashioned letter. It wasn't my plan to vanish into thin air, there was no grand scheme; it just happened.

It wasn't my plan to forget you, the second I walked out of your – our? – door with the two suitcases, never to return. It wasn't my plan to go on to forget you so completely. That wasn't my intent. When you showed up here, without any warning, I didn't recognise you. I tried to hide my bewilderment. Is this how people with amnesia always feel? I stared at you and pretended to know who you were and I said, "Hello, come on in," but I didn't know who you were. And after that, later on, once you were gone (how long did you stay here as an intruder – three days, a whole equinox? How long did it take you to realise that you had no chance of saving me?), it wasn't my plan to forget you over and over. When I started writing to you, just now, I couldn't even remember your name. All the names of the past jostled in my mind, all the men who'd come before you: uncles, lovers, friends, all of them. I couldn't pick your name out of them all. I saw it inside a crowded birdcage, flapping its wings among all the fluttering names of men in my life; my hands could not catch yours. I cleared my head, I gave it my all, I forgot, and suddenly I exclaimed: "George!" Of course. George. I think so. George? George! It's a bit old-fashioned, a bit passé as names go, it's not terribly pretty when written out, but it's yours.

Don't make anything at all of it. It's so easy for us to over-think things. Don't go telling yourself, "I meant so little to him that he forgot me. He doesn't even know my name any more." Sometimes a name is the most unimportant thing. I can remember exactly the way you smell in the morning, for example: musky but otherworldly. If elves had a smell, I think that would be it. And the way you run your hand through your hair. A way that's so *you*, in fact, that if I were in a crowd, and I saw a man up ahead running his hand through his hair in that way, I'd recognise you right there and then, now or in a thousand years. Really, your name isn't all that important. That's still no excuse, though, for my forgetting it even without planning to. When you were here,

I didn't bother to explain. You must have thought that I'd gone mad. I guess that's partly true. You must have seen me like that, with a beard from not picking up a razor for three weeks after so many years clean-shaven. And you probably did notice how tired my eyes were, how sunken they were in their sockets. I feel like I've been squinting constantly ever since I got here. Not to mention how long it's been since I took a shower. The day you came, I hadn't opened my mouth in weeks (I suppose Nawal and I communicate through telepathy). So the first words I said to you, until I had more or less regained use of my voice, were closer to grunts, like a gob of phlegm stuck in my throat that I was trying to spit out, and that must have left an impression.

I should explain. Maybe I ought to start at the beginning, since that's simplest. The beginning is that moment at night's last gasp when I bought a plane ticket, called a cab, packed two huge suitcases, and went to the airport. It happened just like that. No, that's a lie, it was a bit more complicated, a bit more difficult, a bit more underhand.

Actually, that's not the beginning. That's not the right place to start for you to understand. The right place is when Ayub died. Or when I was born. Actually, I'll start with when I was born, sometimes it really is simpler to go in chronological order. That's simplest. I don't want to make too much of it, but the nice thing about that moment is that all the characters in this story are in the same place at the same time. Which is useful. That way, the introductions are made, I can skip all the extra backstory, and then I can do my best to explain, nice and calm, everything that's gone to seed in me. I'll be so bold as to presume you'd still find that interesting.

I was born in the house you came to and found me in two, three weeks ago. When were you here? I barely noticed you, because all I heard were wiswis, a whole racket. Wiswis... nonstop demonic whispering in my ears ever since I came home, there were no distinct words but they were singing death to me, calling me pathetic, complete and total trash. So I saw nothing but wiswis, I heard nothing but wiswis. The minute I made my decision this morning, though, they stopped. Well, they're still there, but they're much quieter, I can barely hear them, it's just a faint buzzing in my ear, music that's verging on the epic, an underground stream reverberating in caverns. It's almost pleasant. But never mind the wiswis. What I was going to tell you about was my being born, wasn't it? Or was it Ayub?

Ayub! Yes, that's it, I wanted to start with Ayub. Remember, one morning, in the dining room, you pointed at a portrait of an unbelievably handsome young man and asked, "Who's this guy?" That's Ayub. My uncle. He was my first friend. And Joséphine was my second. Ayub left us a long time ago, the same time I left this place. Twenty years ago. Or was it twenty-two? It's possible I came back for him. And what if

I did? That wouldn't have been much of a surprise. Ayub is hung high up in the drawing room, next to the portraits of his father and his grandfather.

The day I arrived, I went into the drawing room and Ayub, in his portrait, looked down at me and said, "Is that you? Is that really you? You're all grown up! You're a big guy now! You're not the scared little kid I used to walk down to Joséphine's." He had tears in his eyes, up there, hung up so high, and so did I, down below, tears in my eyes, and he said, "Welcome, come on in, make yourself at home. I've been waiting so long for you, stuck like a fool up here, and I felt so alone without you, and here you are, welcome, come on in, make yourself at home, peace be upon you, my kid, my boy, my boy who's a big guy now," and, I swear, George, you're the only one I'd ever confess this to, that made me so happy that I actually blushed, to be told that I was a big guy. So as soon as I was in there was no getting out, not when Ayub up there had smiled so warmly upon me.

In any case, you have to understand that I didn't know a thing, not when I left, not when I came, I had no idea if I'd be staying. I didn't think a single thing. It's hard to believe, it stands to reason that someone with a good five hours on a plane might have plenty of time to think properly. But I somehow didn't think about anything, not a single thing. I was in a trance.

But that wasn't where I wanted to start, and definitely not where I wanted to end... What was it I said? Right, begin at the beginning. The beginning was a card I got the day before I left. I woke up late that morning. (Were you at work? What's your job again?) I remember two specific details: that I loved you, and that even at that moment you were already more a wisp than a man, as if something had come over me, had already unmoored me from reality.

I woke up and under the door I found an envelope addressed to me. I opened it. Inside was a card written in Arabic. In Arabic! It had been so long since anything of that sort had come in the post. My first thought was that one of my friends was getting married. (But which of my friends, in that faraway world, would have sent me a wedding announcement in Arabic? Which of these children of the diaspora, washed up on a foreign shore, would have taken part in such a charade, pretending that we're from back there when we're so terribly of right here?)

But it was a funeral announcement for Tante Rita. And what was so strange, George, what was so odd and hard to wrap my head around, was that I didn't have a Tante Rita. I didn't have any living aunts left. My aunts and uncles and Ayub and Joséphine were all dead.

This Tante Rita was stuck in my head the whole day. I built her up. I randomly gave her Jeannette's nose and Ayub's eyes. I rounded her out with other features belonging to my family or to myself. Rita became the composite image of a dynasty. Rita naturally had the same quirks I did, a bit overly fond of fresh bread and quality butter, or that habit only we had of wrinkling our nose as we pondered things. At lunch, I thought, "Oh right, yes, of course, she used to play with me when I was a baby." And in the afternoon, I realised, "Oh right, I remember now, Rita who always made me laugh." A bit loopy. A bit too hopped up on pills, but then again anyone who's been through a couple of wars knows the worth of mother's little helper. I recalled her cracking jokes while tossing fresh orange peel into the old stove we gathered around on winter nights. She had tortoiseshell glasses, like Jeannette, and, yes, she wrinkled her nose as she pondered things. In the house I grew up in, there were so many grown-ups and I didn't like them, they were men but they were more like spectres, cold men as faceless as shadows, all clustered together and every so often Ayub pulled away from them to walk me over to Joséphine's. So Rita, a shadow among those shadows, might well have existed, and I might well never have remembered her.

Now I was the only one left. I'd kept a notebook where I'd written down the day on which each member of my family died. I found it that morning, buried deep in a box. I flipped through it. Good god, how many of us there had been, and how many of us were gone! And now we were extinct, just like the dinosaurs. Every generation begat a dozen kids, all to end, once and for all, with me, the only one left, the last one left. And now, out of nowhere, Rita, dead Rita but Rita nonetheless, had burst out of the shadows, had escaped my notebook. I was the last born and now the only one still alive. The man of the house, in fact. A sense of duty began to take root in me, along with an unbearable, morbid curiosity about how Rita had smuggled her way past my oh-so-murderous lines.

Rita lingered in my mind the whole day, like a lizard discovered in a faraway land that turns out to be the missing link with the dinosaurs. So, apparently, they never died out! Their descendant, a spry young reptile, still lives somewhere on the edge of the world. Did you give any thought to that lizard, assuming it exists? I think about it constantly. Poor lizard, poor little lizard. It's born already gone, already prehistoric. It's teetering on the distant shore of history; it counts for nothing. It could be alive but it's just an archaeological curiosity doomed to solitude. And, as the day drew to a close, I found myself thinking about Rita as if I'd known her, as if we'd talked on the phone every day. Oh, she really was a hoot when she called, always with a funny story for me, some little saga, she'd have all the details about the latest village scandal, she'd get such a kick out of blowing them out of proportion for anyone who wanted to listen on the other end of the line, perking up at the smell of fresh coffee with cardamom. Nobody could tell a story like good old Rita, a dyed-in-the-wool spinster of the finest kind, call-her-for-all-the-gossip Rita.

I watched the sun set and tinge pink the city of skyscrapers and metal and glass, and I was surprised to realise I felt sad. I decided that, yes, I needed to go back, for Rita, I was the only one left, I needed to go and make sure that she'd been put in the earth as she ought to be, that she was at rest, peace be upon your soul, Rita. I read and reread the card, tears welling up, the delicate calligraphy of the gilt and spangled letters twirling across gleaming off-white paper.

All that, of course, proved to be Nawal's doing. Yes, I'll begin with Nawal, I told you a bit about her when you were here – Nawal, the lady of the higher hill, Imm Ayub... But wasn't I going to tell you about how I was born? I should explain about my village first.

My village could have been right out of a fairy tale. You've seen yourself just how pretty it is, just how it isn't like all the others. My home's a bit different. Another world, some lost woods between here and tomorrow – that's what Jabalayn is. Something a bit off, it's hard to say what exactly, it's a world that's not quite what's expected, like a fork set a bit too far to the left of the plate, a quality to the air that's imperceptibly *other*.

Jabalayn means "the two hills". You probably remember how, when you got here, this village at the foot of the two hills seemed so small. And how those hills seemed untouchable, tall like two ruthless Amazons guarding the land. On one stands the palace and on the other is Old Jihad's restaurant. Jihad. He's probably dead now. Or living somewhere far away. But if he is, then he must be decrepit. It's odd to think that maybe he's still alive: that means, somewhere in this wide world, there's someone who carries in their soul, whether or not they still dwell on it, the memory of my childhood. Which means that I didn't make anything up – if Old Jihad exists, then so did Jabalayn.

Jihad had a restaurant. That's the odd thing you saw on the lower hill. I went over to his place every day. Sometimes on my own, often with Ayub and Joséphine. When we were over there, I could believe that Ayub was my father and Joséphine my mother, and we were a happy family living in a house surrounded by flowers at the bottom of the valley. Old Jihad loved to tell me the story of his restaurant. He repeated it so often that I can remember every last detail as if the story were my own. That's how it usually was in my family. We passed stories around and around until we'd internalised them so completely that we could no longer tell what was ours and what wasn't.

One morning in 1966, Jihad, who wasn't Old Jihad yet, woke up in a good mood. He'd alway say, and stress, "in '66," before shouting, "son of sixty-six whores!" It'd been ages since he'd last woken up in a good mood. He rolled out of bed foggy-headed and dry-mouthed and swore to himself that he was never, ever drinking arak again. Jihad was in a good mood because the stubborn vestiges of alcohol that morning had driven home that he was done. Done with everything: this future drained of promise, this land gone to seed, this village full of idiots. Done with waking up every morning to this pounding headache and to this life on the lower hill where, every morning, he'd go and open his small place for the earliest risers to come at dawn and enjoy hummus for breakfast: old fogeys missing all their teeth who hadn't slept a wink, day labourers set on filling their bellies before they were off to work in the city (that was before they were forced to work in the settlements), teenagers stumbling in from a night out. Old Jihad's hour, his bulwark, his home, was the early morning. Dawn was like a rocket blast-off for the day. At one in the afternoon, having cleared the kitchen and wiped all the tables, Old Jihad would take a nap for an hour. In the evening, he could be found on the front steps of his house, drinking and telling anyone who'd listen his opinions of the world, which changed with the daily paper's headlines, and which boiled down to insulting invisible others: them, us, foreigners, or even, sometimes and sacrilegiously, God. But God was just as often his ally, the one he called on to send folks – them, us, foreigners, women, children, men, leaders, elites, layabouts, all those stupid shitty whores, sometimes even him – straight to hell.

So he came to the conclusion that he was done with all that. He wasn't made for village life. What a cruel joke fate had played on him for him to be born here, when he was so hungry for the whole world out there. His entrepreneurial spirit was trapped in a shithole village. But he wasn't about to go and put down roots somewhere else: America was kind of a mess and his cousin who'd moved to some dump not far from Chicago was really having a hard time of it. All alone in that huge country halfway around the world! Europe was for the snootiest snobs. (If Ayub was around while he was ranting, he'd add, warmly: "Oh, it's perfect for guys just like you. Me, on the other hand – what the fuck am I doing in Vienna or Paris?") And don't get him started on Asia or Africa! For a couple of minutes, he'd seriously considered putting a bullet through his head. But that wasn't really his style. He'd tell me this every time, repeating all over again, hissing through his teeth, pensively, "Fucking son of sixty-six whores." Then he'd clarify, gesturing at the restaurant, "Don't you ever give in to that temptation." What Jihad needed was to leave this land. He was convinced that if he'd been born in another country, a "de-vel-oped and tech-no-log-i-cal-ly ad-vanced coun-try", he'd have been an astro-naut. He should have been the first man on the moon. Just his luck! Here, simply getting to the far end of the village was enough of a hassle – forget the moon! He'd start saying over and over, up until his death, "When apricots blossom, Palestine will be free."

"When apricots blossom" is a turn of phrase we have: apricots are in flower for so short a time that "when apri-cots blossom" means almost never. A nice authentic peas-ant expression, that. You have to admit it's more elegant than anything about hens having teeth or pigs flying. I can't claim to know much about farming, not even how to grow courgettes, but apricots – I know apricots. The murmur of apricots, the music of their blossoming, the aroma of this climate concentrated into an elixir in their flesh.

Old Jihad was saying that there was more of a chance of him, Old Jihad, son of Ahmad, landing on Mars than of us having freedom, when apricots blossom, son of sixty-six whores.

There weren't really any restaurants in Jabalayn, let alone in the surrounding hamlets. Old Jihad's place was something special: the only spot of its sort for kilometres around. There would always be a familiar face there, but also plenty of new ones come from the south or the north or the west or the east to eat here. Jihad had struck gold with his hummus joint. Riches that he barely touched: his older son was married and living in Jerusalem, and his wife was the frugal sort. Each morning, as he set about making fresh hummus before sunrise, he told himself that this money would be useful for something. He had, he would always say with a raised finger, "big dreams". It wasn't for nothing, after all, that he'd named his youngest daughter Ahlam. But up to that day when he woke up in a good mood, he had been hard-pressed to say what those ahlam of his were. He didn't want his wife or his body or his job to be different. All three already suited him just fine. Or didn't suit him, that wasn't important, that wasn't the problem, he didn't really care about that. Anyway, he woke up in a good mood: he took in his house – stone, stone, could that possibly *be* any bulkier and uglier – and the restaurant tacked onto the house – stone, stone, more stone. And he felt sheer contempt for the stone and for the olive trees – what ugly things! – and for his life – what a disappointment! – and for this when-apricots-blossom that would do him in. The problem was the stone and the olive trees, yes, and the apricots and this accursed, unchanging landscape. How could he dream in such a plain, stark landscape that forced him to contemplate who he was, that stood as an unassailable "No!" to any change he might wish for? He pondered that for the whole day. Green then white then green then white, he could no longer take this place changing and changing its mind about whether to be desert sand or verdant land – what fickleness, what ugliness, he'd had enough of these curves and these stones and this green and this white until apricots blossomed.

Back then, Jihad, relatively young Jihad, would come to our place every week, arms laden with trays of hummus, to watch the news on TV. Jeannette and he were good friends. (How? Why? This jolly man with a damp moustache and hard-nosed Jeannette – *friends*? It was a total mystery.) Jeannette, settled comfortably on her father's gilt sofa, extolled armed struggle, as had her mother before her. Jihad, in turn, thought that it was completely pointless and that these refined ladies didn't know the first thing about any of it. And he'd felt a fatherly tenderness toward Ayub from the outset. That evening, as a presenter kept on yammering about something he had no idea about in a language he didn't understand and as Jeannette kept on prattling, he noticed something in the background of the show. He deduced that the odd thing on screen was a restaurant. What a strange building. No question of it, that was a restaurant, but like a spaceship too. "Quiet!" he said to Jeannette as he leaned forward to get a better look. The stone, the damn stone, the hateful stone, had made way for huge bay windows. The building's roof was at an angle that seemed completely impractical for life on Earth. But totally practical for lift-off. A dome – in all likelihood useless – perched atop the roof. And capping off this vision was a sign perhaps symbolising the birth of a star, an explosion, adrift in front of the restaurant, an invitation to an intergalactic journey. At once a rocket and a space colony. What genie or genius had conjured up such a thing? That was exactly what Jihad needed, son of sixty-six whores: to live in space here on this prison of an Earth. What a fantasy, he thought: if he couldn't go to the moon, and he couldn't leave this accursed land, then he'd bring the moon here. When apricots are blossoming, when time is meaningless, then the whole damn universe is the limit.

In the wake of that epiphany, Jihad spent three years remodelling his house and his restaurant. Word had it that in the mornings he could be found yelling at the day labourers (the very ones who ate breakfast there), calling them good-for-nothings and thieves. And so they just worked even more slowly. Meanwhile, his wife left him ("for nobody whatsoever," she would announce, "thank you very much") to while away her life happily with her parents one village over, in a house of sturdy stone, where it stayed cold in the summer and warm in the winter. Jihad barely noticed his wife's departure or their children's pleas. None of that mattered: after three years, on a nice winter day, his space-bound restaurant was ready. Buttressed against the cliff, the spaceship was akin to a mutant trying to extricate itself from the bowels of the earth. He'd tacked the adjective "panoramic" onto the name of the restaurant, which hung above the valley, while the rest of the structure curved back to the mountain's peak, where a dome of concrete had pride of place. He was all alone now, but damn if he didn't have a rocket at last!

In the afternoons, Old Jihad would bring me a Coke and tell me that we were sitting pretty in the spaceship that would take him away one day. "Away anywhere, so long as it's far away. Yes, my boy, you're in the belly of the blaster. Careful, if you make me mad, I'll push the button and woosh, I'll shoot into the sky!" And so Old Jihad's dream, his flying saucer of stone, was primed, ready for a launch that, sixty years on, still hadn't come. And Ayub, Joséphine, and I all called him Abu al-Sarukh: Old Father Rocket.

Don't get the wrong idea about my situation. I'm fine. Things are fine. Being alone does me good. Time's thickening, it's actually turning palpable and sonorous, it's taken on the form of a huge blanket I could wrap around myself. If time flows, it flows like a fountain. Sometimes I can even taste it.

It's true that I'm losing the sense of weeks and months. Days, though, seem to have a body to them, each day different from the last, each one a fellow traveller. The village lies fallow at the bottom of the hill. We're not really connected by road to the rest of the country; it's a long and bumpy drive through mountains to get to Jabalayn. Every day Nawal comes to tell me that the settlers are circling the city in the distance with their jeeps. Vultures ready to swoop down on us.

Every day I sit on the terrace and I look at this besieged land; the horizon is hazy, like a daydream I'm struggling to draw out. It's hard to keep my eyes open. It's nice to live in this half-light.

As soon as you got here, you said, "I came to find you."
I barely heard you. The wiswis grew even louder when you
stepped through the door. The house was repulsed by you.
The whispering spread through the drawing room to drive
you out. To find me, but why? Wiswiswis the cut stones
cracked before my eyes and out of these cracks came whispers: wiswiswis. The house shook but you, you were sitting
in front of me, not moving, nothing but affectionate and
good-hearted. You listened as I told you my problems. "They
can be solved," you said gently. Wiswiswis your words were
drowned in these oceans of whispers.

You were aghast. That I do remember. And you were
astonishingly kind: you did not scold me for anything,
not at first. You were too worried. "Has it been two weeks
now that you've been here all by yourself? Two weeks!
Whatever have you been doing? How have you been keeping yourself fed?" Wiswiswis... how to answer you in this
thundering onslaught of whispers? (I had my hands over
my ears but the stones kept on cracking and the house kept
on shaking.)

If I were you, my first question would have been: "How
could you do that to me?" But I don't know who you are,
let alone how to answer you: two weeks? A whole equinox?
Three months? Two days?

Nawal saw you in the rental car heading into the village. When she isn't cooking, she stands sentry on the terrace. Hours monitoring the horizon, a watchtower unto herself. In the deserted village, your car – so red! so preposterously loud! – stood out immediately. Nawal rushed to my bedroom, pounded at my door, "Faysal! Faysal! There's someone! A settler! Someone, it's a disaster!" She dragged me out to the terrace to watch from afar as your figure made its way up the mountain. "Faysal, get a rolling pin, grab a pitchfork, just be ready, good Lord, do something!"

You rang, I opened the door, and there you were, looking sheepish. And then you gave me a smile, ever so slowly, and that smile of yours must have lasted a full ten minutes at least. You'd taken a plane and then driven here, to the middle of nowhere, just for me. And I didn't remember you. You'd combed through all my notebooks, all the scribblings I'd left around our house. And so you'd pieced together that I had come back home and so you'd called all my friends, dug through my past (what was left of it, what was still in reach), followed lead after lead, and you'd unearthed an address (no easy matter, you would point out, in a land where streets don't have names), and got here, only to see that I'd forgotten your name. "May I come in?" you asked.

I wasn't averse to this handsome man, this familiar-looking man, coming in, but I wanted to tell him, "Wait, if you come in, you'll fall into Nawal's trap. You won't leave anytime soon." But that would have taken too long to explain and you weren't listening.

So for two weeks, or two years, or a whole equinox, I've been on the brink of leaving, but I just can't bring myself to. There's Ayub up high – he's not much of a talker, but he's looking down on me with a kindliness I haven't seen before. And she's here too, and, as wheezy as she might be, it'd just about break my heart to abandon her and leave her all alone again in this massive empty house on the top of a hill deep within an equally empty village. Even in her loneliness she'd have gone on preparing banquets for a homecoming never to come.

What isn't empty, though, is the horizon with its growing number of settlements. When I came back here, two weeks or a whole equinox ago, they were just a thin, barely perceptible line on the horizon. Jabalayn has always been a secluded village and so it's been spared the worst. But now the settlers have started closing in, getting nearer with each day. It boggles the mind how swiftly a settlement can be erected. It's easy, just build it in the same old way: a hundred identical houses, all of them ugly. Now, from the conservatory or the terrace, I can see the windows, and, at night when the lights are all on, I can make out heads and silhouettes. Which made it possible for me to decide. That's why I'm writing to you today. The settlers will reach Jabalayn soon; a few days, at most. They'll make their way into the ghost town. They'll move triumphantly into the houses. They'll say: "They weren't here." The town's capture will be swift and barely remarked upon. Then they'll look up. They'll see, to the east, mournfully adrift in the sky, a spaceship devoid of astronauts. To the west, a palace. And they'll venture up. They'll see the rotting corpse of one of their own, and, inside, she or he who killed him.

That's why Nawal summoned me. She can't do anything about it herself. She thinks that my presence here might scare them off. She'd have liked for me to get a gun and sit on the terrace each morning, ready to shoot at any oncoming settler or soldier, to safeguard the family home. For me to be a man, a real man.

Every night, Nawal goes through the house three times, checks that each window is properly shut, each door locked. She inspects every darkened corner, every closet, no doubt worried that, should she let her defences down, something might jump out and swallow her world whole. She goes out into the garden and rummages through each shrub, to flush out the danger lurking within.

I have to tell you more about the morning I left. I wasn't aware of anything about my homeland any more. I did have some back and forth with the lawyer who— hold on, that can wait. Now isn't the time to talk about the lawyer. I didn't know what was happening. I'd gone and deleted every app and blocked every media outlet that might update me on what's so very tactfully referred to, where you are, as "the situation". I'd told myself that I needed a break. As you've no doubt heard, what they call their "offensive" broke out several months ago. Here's a little secret: they think they're God's cowboys. The "offensive" they keep talking about is the day the settlers who'd already been occupying a large section of the West Bank decided that they were done waiting and it was time to strike. Their D-Day, I guess: they were going to take what they could of the territory, and take it by force. They rolled into the Palestinian towns, it was so easy, they just had to come in guns blazing, shoot a few dozen dead, and boom. It started out as a small-time guerrilla operation. Then, because they were so well organised, they assembled some sort of Judea–Samaria Armed Forces. They went all in, city by city, town by town, no holds barred. The world looked away; forgot that we existed. The countries around us actually approved: they let out a sigh of relief, rid at last of the most troublesome people of the century. The West Bank, this bit of land that doesn't so much as have a recognised country name or status on the world stage, is a battlefield. Seeing how successful the operations were, more and more Israelis not living in the settlements joined the Judea–Samaria Armed Forces. They're fanatics. They felt like they could go right ahead and be themselves at last: a settler is just an Israeli whose mask of propriety has come off. And, in the end, they took almost all of it. They moved in everywhere. As I write to you, there are still a few remote spots like Jabalayn that haven't fallen into Armed Forces hands yet: our last pitiable bastions. The official army left them be. I'd bet the army's helping them (the same way that I'm pretty sure all the countries around us secretly are). On the radio, Israeli commentators wring their hands about what these military tactics say about Israel's democratic integrity ("Oh, *now* they're worried," Nawal says to the radio, which still doesn't reply).

Well, where was I? I wanted to tell you about my birth. I'm writing to you, actually, because I'm scared of being misunderstood. That's the worst thing possible. I don't want you getting the wrong idea. I didn't talk much when you were here. Because I didn't know what to say. I'm making up for that now. It's not dying I'm scared of, it's being misunderstood. The Armed Forces will be here soon. Maybe the man I killed was a scout. They must be looking for him. Does it take long for a body to rot? Should I hide him, bury him? No, let him lie there under the almond trees, his ugliness bared to the sky. That's my one act of resistance. It doesn't make any difference. Every morning, Nawal tells me they're coming, they're here, they're at the door. She's gone mad, they're not here yet, they're busy in actual cities and actual villages taking the lives and slitting the throats of whoever they come across. They'll get here later on. I've got all the time in the world.

When you were here, you made me coffee and talked like nothing was wrong. You'd learned how to make Arabic coffee (it took such attention, watching the coffee's surface like this, and I never did have the focus you did). You were surprised to find the kitchen fully stocked, the pantry overflowing with provisions, the table set and ready for us to dig in, at noon and then at eight. You read the spice labels out loud: cardamom, sumac, cinnamon, saffron. You opened the fridge – an ancient thing, with that bisque hue like all old fridges, and you were shocked at the amount of fresh produce. (Where did the meat come from? The lamb? The yoghurt? What about those yellow and red and green sauces? You didn't dare to ask me but you called out what you saw.) You talked loudly, to fill the house's emptiness. You stayed put in front of the fridge, inspecting the aubergine and labneh and eggs and goat's cheese in brine and tomatoes and courgettes, as if doing so would allow you to solve the mystery of their presence. And then you settled in. The next day, you handed me your razor. "That beard doesn't really suit you," you said.

As I shaved carefully in the bathroom, Nawal stood behind me, dying of curiosity.

"Who – what – *why* did he come here? Is he going to haul you off? He can't, he absolutely can't. Those settlers will be here any day now, and the whole army after that. Then the border will be here, right here. It'll all be over. You want to live a long life somewhere else as a deserter? No, better for you to die here, on this higher hill."

I clicked my tongue and whispered, "Enough! Not now. Leave me alone."

While I shaved, you took the rental car and went to find a store. You came back and said, "All right, tonight we're eating on the terrace." You'd bought tomatoes, cucumbers, onions, and meat. (Why didn't you use what was in the fridge on the first night? Were you scared the food had been cursed?) You spent the afternoon cooking and Nawal watched you. She reluctantly told me that you did have the knack for it. That evening, I came back to myself. I remember it, I recognised you and talked to you. The sun set. You set up a table, draped a white tablecloth embroidered along the hem with blue flowers, you opened some wine, and we ate, and we drank. Something, I can't remember what, with a pronounced flavour of mint. Nawal watched us. I got the impression that Old Jihad's place was lit up and blazing with a thousand fires; as if nothing had changed since the sixties. And, from the world of my great-grandfather's villa, I looked at Old Jihad's UFO and thought about the other, calmer life that I could have lived, here, with you. The flowers in the garden and the trees had regained their density, their contours. The air had the freshness of an Eden, and I could see the trajectory of the sturdy, real existence that we could have led here together. We'd have worked in the city, in Nablus. We'd have driven to work each morning in your red car, windows down to enjoy the crisp morning air. And in the evenings, the city, receding in its valley, would look like a constellation as we reached our welcoming, resplendent house, remade in our image, a haven of peace and love. On the weekends we'd have tended to our vegetable patch. We'd have invited friends to come and live in the village. It would have come back to life like an ailing heart as fresh blood is pumped through.

The house we had our backs to, however, was simply a house: habitable, unremarkable. It stood for nothing what-soever. It was a house you and I happened to live in, and it was sweet. I stared at the UFO and, behind me, I could see the open windows of all three storeys of the palace. At that moment, with you who had come from the other end of the world to this place at the edge of nothing, the prospect of return didn't just feel possible; it felt desirable.

And my eyes dropped down: between the two hills, in the valley's depths, was where the witch Joséphine's house lay. Another landscape entirely: as if descending from the hill's peak to its base meant descending to another latitude, another country, another universe entirely. As a child, when Ayub was still here, I raced down Old Jihad's hill after drink-ing my Coke to see the witch and my uncle in their magical kingdom. Before the sun set, I went up the higher hill and returned to the cold, self-important world that the men of my family had been so foolhardy as to build.

I really wanted, on this evening, to take you to the witch's house, to show you what remained of it. Night fell: a lake of blackness between me and Old Jihad's place, which I imagined all lit up. Down below, invisible, translucent, forgotten by all apart from myself and Old Jihad should he still be alive, lay the memory of the witch's house. I wanted to take you so that a shred of this memory might live in you also.

One night, Nawal, worried, came to see me in my room.

"Faysal, he wants our money!"

"Who does?"

"Your... your friend."

"I don't understand. What money?"

She spread her arms wide.

"All this! These things, this house."

"Let me sleep."

"Foreigners are all the same. I'm one to know. How many do you think I've seen in my life? Consuls, ambassadors, directors, businessmen – leeches. They come and drink my whisky and eat my bread; when the conversation turns to Palestine, they say, 'Well, I never' and 'What a shame,' then they leave without a word, without anything to remember them by. Stay here. Defend this house on the higher hill or die here. Wake up."

You shouldn't blame Nawal. It's not that she doesn't like you. In her mind, you're meaningless, a mere footnote. And she prefers to keep matters in the family. Our house is about to be taken, along with my life. Such things are done in private. Even from her perch, in an empty village that's already gone, Nawal can't stop fretting over what people might say. I remind her that there are no people left who might say anything. She retorts that it's the principle of the thing. That even if she were the last soul alive, she'd still comport herself with dignity and grace.

To die here: the thought does please me at times. You may have sensed as much, Jabalayn's lushness, a fairyland where Old Jihad's restaurant, now overrun by bramble and foxglove, is wreathed with an unearthly halo of fireflies weaving around the house's almond trees, unmooring us from reality.

The settlers always had weapons. Those legions of high-tech Athenas were born armed with shields and spears, rifles and assault tanks. A race of soldiers. They hurtled down the hills they occupied and took the big cities, then the villages. They made short work of the southern cities. They seized Hebron in a matter of hours. The army said, "We don't understand, we did our best to restrain them," but I know they were helping them. From the southern cities, they pressed northward; in no time, they'd scoured the whole land. At first, they steered clear of the cities the foreigners were fond of. If they invaded Bethlehem, they'd be stirring up a hornets' nest; that would have to wait. Likewise for those ghost towns such as Jabalayn nowhere to be found on world maps. But now they've taken Bethlehem and the terribly concerned foreigners have simply said: "Well, I never" and "What a shame."

I can hear them in the distance. They don't dare enter yet. They're nervous. Jabalayn scares them: at dawn the two hills are two eagles hunched over their nest; at dusk, two sleeping ogres. They must have already seen the palace lit up at night. For several days now, Nawal has forbidden me to turn on the lights. "At your orders, Imm Ayub," I find myself saying sarcastically. (Sarcasm may be the one weapon, the one prerogative I've clung to; I still obey all her orders even so.) Since then, we sit in the dark and do not talk. We wait.

Often, like some apathetic teenager, I hole up in my room. I listen to music. I stare at the ceiling. Sometimes I emerge, I go outside, laptop under my arm. It's amazing that I can have a computer, that I can still use it here. I take a seat outside, at the table where we used to eat, and I write to you – like an idle, bored boyfriend, pining constantly for you. As if I were writing to you because words were the only way I had to get you, to catch you in my glittering net... missives sent not to reach out to you but to ensnare you and bring you under my control.

It's true that, while you were here, I hardly spoke. Even when I tried my hardest, words barely got out of my mouth. I couldn't utter them, I couldn't even make a sound with my throat; it felt like I'd forgotten this fundamental bodily operation. When the wiswis surround me, I actually forget how to breathe. And you scared Nawal, too. She sees you as a sign of the end. She wanted you to leave right away. You didn't even see the whole house, there wasn't time. I made up your room next to mine. I couldn't have you sleeping in my bed; Nawal would have gone insane. No, I'm wrong: it's Nawal, the consummate hostess, who made up your room.

For ten years I was with you and not once did I speak of this country or this house. And for ten years you politely consented not to know anything. See, I do remember that we spent ten years together. Not all is forgotten. The memories come back as Nawal and I sit in the darkness with our ears pricked up for the least crack of a dry leaf or a Kalashnikov shot in the distance.

Sometimes, to break up this unbearable silence, she tells me stories. She never really directs them at me; I think she talks so as not to forget. One time she couldn't decide what to make up, so she went and told the story of Little Red Riding Hood.

"There was or there was not, in a time long past, a little girl by the name of Layla..." Then, with the upbeat tone one uses with children, she asked me: "Layla who?"

I laughed and replied, mimicking a child's voice: "Layla the Red!"

"Very good! Layla the Red went to visit her teta, who lived... where?"

"In the woods!"

"Bravo! So Layla went into the woods, stopped to gather flowers, ate the sandwich that her mother had made for her under an almond tree while listening to the burble of the stream running nearby, but... who was hiding in the shadows and watching her?"

"The... the wolf!"

"That's right, the wolf. And what did this wolf want?"

"He wanted to eat her!"

"That he did, and so he followed her. Layla got lost. Then, as she was trying to pick between two paths in front of her, the wolf stopped and..." She paused.

"He told her to take the longer path!"

"Yes, he did! So Layla took the long way around, while the wolf ran to the house of her teta. He ate the woman up, he put on her clothes, and he waited for her... And then she showed up! She went inside the house of her teta. 'Teta, what big hands you have. Teta, what big eyes you have. Teta, what big feet you have. Teta, what big teeth you have.' And then what happened?"

"The, uh..." I paused.

"Don't tell me you forgot!"

"The wolf..."

"The wolf ate – her – right – up!"

And Nawal pounced on me as if she were going to eat *me* right up.

I'd left Jabalayn behind. I'd torn out my roots as thoroughly as I could, and set them ablaze. No, that's not true, all this about roots, that's bullshit. What roots? What I have are hooks sunk deep in my neck to keep me in place. When I try to move, they yank at my skin and I bleed.

After the blaze, I'd been dragged from boarding school to boarding school in Europe. Such is the privilege of the rich: they send their children not to prison but to the mountains. All the while, in Jabalayn, everyone was dropping like flies. Our sprawling family tree shrivelled up at terrifying speed. Old age, metastatic cancers, heart attacks: every member of my family snuffed out, one by one. Humiliating deaths, too, without the least bit of fight, not a single martyr. Measly illnesses. My teenage mind devised a theory that some divine entity, clearly baleful, yet exquisitely mannered, had deemed us reprehensible, filthy, disgraceful, and, rather than show its hand so openly by smiting us all at once, preferred to obliterate us little by little through organ failure. In a notebook, I jotted down the names, dates, places, and causes of death for the whole dynasty. At that moment, for so many of them, they ceased to be cold shadows and became individuals. Just look at this small sampling:

Edward, heart attack, Miami (USA)

Henri, lung cancer, Khartoum (Sudan)

Margot, Alzheimer's?, London (UK)

Edward (2), heart attack, Jabalayn

Victoria, suicide?, Jabalayn

Manya, pancreatic cancer, Benghazi (Libya)

Henry (≠ Henri), brain cancer, Jabalayn

Juana, mysterious circumstances, New Orleans (USA)

Antoine, throat cancer, Beirut (Lebanon)

George, heart attack, Jabalayn

Elisabeth, heart attack, Jabalayn

Madeleine, heart attack, Jabalayn

Marguerite, heart attack, Jabalayn

I was waiting my turn. When Tante Jeannette died, not long after I left, I was convinced I was next. There was an implacable divine logic to it. It was the maid who came back from holiday only to find Jeanette with her tortoiseshell glasses on her head, her stern face unmoving, sitting in the same chair I had you, you the stranger, sit in when you came. I wonder if she'd begun to rot in this chair. She'd certainly rotted enough while she was alive. So I staked out this very rot in myself, too; every morning, I checked my pulse, took my temperature, did breathing exercises to make sure my lungs still worked. In the evenings, I repeated the ritual: pulse, temperature, breathing exercises. Any variation at all, any irregularity would confirm my impending death.

And yet I'm still here. This cruel god seems to have had his fill of punishment; my family is finally purified. Or I'm not even worth the hassle. On my worst days, I wonder if he's decided that it's a far better punishment to leave me here, alone. "That'll teach you," someone up there must have decided. Or maybe not even that: what uncalled-for torture that would be, to leave me abandoned thus like an unfortunate lizard. The last-of, the last-to.

I'd never contemplated a return to my native land. I was happy where I was, in this European country that's a bit unreal the way all European countries tend to be, and then there was you, and I had no friends or family in this distant land, remote, slowly vanishing into the mist. I figured it was best to do my mourning before the fact. Then, who knows, I could say, "Come on, let's live in Palestine, shall we, in Jabalayn? You'll see, it's nice, there's nothing there. I have a big house. You'll laugh, the house is really something, everyone calls it 'the palace' and it sprawls out over a huge hill that looks like an Amazon warrior. My great-grandfather So-and-So was the one to start building it in the twenties, he wanted a palace but it was really his son, my grandfather Ibrahim, the famous Abu Ayub, who made the house into the ghastly misshapen creature it is now. Oh, you'll love it, George, you don't know the particular fantasy that Palestinian men have. So-and-So had a huge house built on the highest hill of Jabalayn. 'There are two hills in this village? Well, we'll go for the higher one.' And up there, where it really isn't that practicable to live, So-and-So built his dream, a huge birthday cake in stone. When they came by cab, our guests told the driver that they were going to Qasr al-Jabalayn, the palace on the two hills."

So-and-So... I'm sorry, I really am, I don't remember his name any more, but I'll tell you this: he had seven kids, five girls and two boys, one being Ibrahim, and they all lived together in the same house and so did their own children. I can't remember all their names. And it was when this great-grandfather whose name I've forgotten died, and Ibrahim stepped into the limelight, that this family's history became capital-H History.

I never personally knew this famous Ibrahim. He died in the early eighties at a very advanced age and after a very admirable life, leaving behind Nawal, who followed him soon after, and his three adult children: Jeannette, my mother, and Ayub. Some of his sisters got married, and trapped their husbands in the shadows of the palace on the higher hill. The earliest years of my life were spent in the women's dark quarters where, in the afternoons, some would sit down to knit scarves and caps for ghost children while others would gather like flies in the kitchen. And the men would stay in the drawing room for hours, not talking. Even now I wonder what these men did so as not to talk: were they in deep meditation? Or did they just not have anything to talk about, apart from an occasional dumb joke, the odd bit of hare-brained political analysis? In any case, they were all cold to me, apart from Ayub. I hated them and I do think they felt the same about me. When you were here, could you smell the lingering odour of rot and ruin that not even bleach could cover up?

Ibrahim: we called him, deferentially, Abu Ayub. "Father of Ayub", just as Nawal is Imm Ayub, "Mother of Ayub". This is how men and their wives are known, by the first name of their oldest son. Now, because I've been living in these depths for ages and ages, I feel like I know Abu Ayub inside and out. Here I am, alone, in his house, a hideaway teetering on some rock and on the edge of a cliff, trapped in my palace on the higher hill. Whenever I think about leaving, since I do still think about it, the whispers resurface wiswiswis and drown out my brain. At night, I see life go on in the distance; down there, while the sunset drains away the day's colour, the settlements' lights twinkle with the confidence of the victorious. On this side, Old Jihad's restaurant is no longer aglow. My imagination, left to its own devices, dreams that it shines on like a lighthouse in the darkness, illuminating the dark ocean all around. The restaurant was abandoned after the fire. Rats run between the tables, snakes wedge themselves comfortably in the scarlet cabinets, hyenas have already chewed through the cushions' fabric. Part of the ceiling must have caved in. The restaurant's lights are only in my head. Down there, far off, the settlements' lights taunt me: there are so many, they're having family dinners, maybe they'll come out after for a night-time stroll. It's so nice out right now, it's early spring, the end of winter, you get the idea. And they don't even realise that in the dark hills facing them, I alone watch them, envy them, hate them.

Just among ourselves, we called the village al-Bizayn, the two boobs. And the house was the palace on the bigger boob. "Ourselves" meaning Joséphine, Ayub, and me.

The elder son, Ibrahim's big brother – I don't remember his name. A poor guy who went crazy at thirty and committed suicide. One night, he hanged himself from one of the almond trees. They found him at dawn, shrouded in the scent of flowers, swaying gently in the wind. His body was reddening with the dawn light. (In the house's hallways, the cold shadows murmured, whenever I was in my room for too long or away at Joséphine's too long, that I was no different from him.) After that, Ibrahim became the man of the house. That had to be a real blow for him, having grown up thinking he would have it easy, no family responsibilities, that was his big brother's problem, and then boom, without even a second to mourn his brother, to learn or make sense of things, he was thrust into his place at the helm.

He did a good job of it, I have to say. Who would have thought: the baby of the family, the spoiled baby, who preferred plump cushions and sweet wine, the one with the soft skin of a fresh-faced child, the fine traits of a Christian icon, the limp wrists of a pampered scion, the one who spent his early adulthood waltzing from European capital to European capital; who would have thought, the one everyone expected to become an antiques dealer in Vienna, that one, in fact, had an obscene, diabolical business sense. All through my childhood I was told and told about Ibrahim's brilliance: apparently they called him pasha in Tripoli and

Istanbul, lord in Manchester and Lausanne. Jeannette bored me to tears rattling off all his honorifics, and all the heads of state and other kings and princes who had come and stayed at the palace on the higher hill (yes, yes, in Jabalayn where you were, George, you slept in the same bed that Ethiopian princesses once did). One prince, she said, had even come with a procession of elephants that climbed up the hill.

Ibrahim had plenty of dealings and the house had metamorphosed accordingly; as his wealth multiplied, so the house ballooned. His dealings in Qatar paid for the conservatory at the back of the house. Nowadays, it's just a dilapidated structure overrun by brambles, but back then, oh, there had been three gardeners and every plant in the world within. Ibrahim loved flowers. His dealings in Chile made the back garden possible. After a stint in Italy where he travelled with the man Nawal only ever called "that priest", the two syllables spat out with barely veiled disdain, Ibrahim decided that the house could use some pretty columns and that's why, on the terrace, you have a colonnade of utterly useless Roman pillars in marble.

Each drawing room – there are six, can you believe it, *six*? – was a universe unto itself. There was a vaguely ancient Greek room; just the thought of it makes me blush. So many ridiculous frescoes of banquets, paintings of the Acropolis... how on earth could he have looked at that and thought, "Yes, yes, that's a wonderful idea!" There was the Jaffa room and its famous paintings depicting, across three walls, the history of the land, and, on the fourth, the sea.

The Paris room I'll let you imagine for yourself. There was a drawing room that he called Alexandria, and then there was the Arcadia room, which I'd only ever seen in tatters but where naive depictions of shepherds and shepherdesses can still be made out, lying on the banks of pastel-hued rivers, under apple trees, kissing or playing the flute. Why he'd left it to moulder, I never dared to ask. Nawal often told me, "If you don't count Paris, he's recreated the Mediterranean here." I hadn't realised the Mediterranean could be so ugly. And then there was his office. His *study* – he affected that English word – which he'd had erected behind the green-house (a fanciful configuration that nobody had ever questioned) and which not a soul, not even after his death, was to enter.

We rarely made use of those drawing rooms; even now, although I don't have much to do, I've never ventured in except to dust a bit here and there. We only ever met in the sitting room (that was the opposite of ornamentation: a simple room carved out of the massive stone with floral-print armchairs in plastic slipcovers). On some winter nights, we'd indulge ourselves with tea in the Jaffa room. But in Nawal and Ibrahim's heyday, whenever Imm and Abu Ayub threw a party, the house came to life. The most esteemed guests (in order of importance: ambassadors, then poets and businessmen, then priests and professors) were received, needless to say, in the Jaffa room, the things-were-better-back-then room, and they all pretended they were swanning by the sea. The most annoying guests – "that priest", for example, but also women past their prime and bachelors, sons of good families who didn't work a day in their lives, those with too many political opinions and those who didn't have enough – were all relegated to the Paris room where a watercolour Sacré-Cœur watched over them. The two kitchens bustled with cooks, servants, waiters, the invisible buttresses of Ibrahim and Nawal's legendary parties. They were the talk of the whole land. Even the Israelis who heard about them were jealous of those inconceivable parties at the palace on the higher hill. Reportedly some went so far as to try to sneak in. For a few hours on those nights, Nawal and Ibrahim conjured up a land of plenty. And the memory of them endured long after their death: I grew up in the shadows of those bygone parties. I lived here in the sorry hour after the party's end, when the gloom of loneliness descends upon the hosts now alone in the garden as they pick up napkins and blow out candles.

I went to the village school (all the way at the entrance to Jabalayn, across from the cemetery: a square block of concrete open to the sky). Of course, I also had a tutor at home, an old man with a doctorate in something totally dull and utterly European, probably Latin or maybe medieval metaphysics. He was supposed to "teach languages" first.

Nor did that education stop when I was in the women's quarters: one or another of those cold shadows would regularly pull away from the bunch to lead me into a dark, chilly corner of the house and have me spend hours on end reviewing the horrible French subjunctive or those elusive English irregular verbs.

The tutor's responsibility after that was to inculcate me with the cultural knowledge lacking at the village school, which consisted, essentially, of long, laborious translations of pointless texts. Translations from Greek and Latin, as if I were supposed to have been raised in another era and another country. I forget the tutor's name but I still shudder at the memory of declensions hammered into my head over interminable winter nights.

The history of Palestine, however, might as well be a family story. Each of the shadows entrusted a bit of it to me with a whisper, like an opal they placed in my hands. I understood what they told me so quickly and thoroughly that before long they all came to think of me as both scribe and shrink: I was the boy to whom they could confess the traumas they would never dare to utter to one another. I was the receptacle for their fears and worries. They were so willing to inter their injuries in me that I would live the rest of my life feeling like a walking open wound.

I was never taught Palestine; it was cast upon me like a curse.

I fell asleep yesterday after telling you about Palestine as if it were a curse. Bullshit. I've just woken up. It's noon. I've got a splitting headache. I drink a lot these days, to kill time. Just now, I dragged myself from my bedroom to the kitchen. I needed coffee. In the hallway, I stopped to take in Ayub's portrait. His eyes were like pure black flames and he looked at me reprovingly. Nawal was already awake. She didn't even notice me as she brushed past and glanced at Ayub before letting out a long sigh.

Once, mornings in this house overflowed with worlds that shimmered, promises that unfurled before me in all their sweep. The future, in my childhood, held the particular tenor of a dream you actually believed and could almost sink your teeth into. It had the density of clay one could hold and form. And, little by little, it lost this particular consistency and turned misty; the future's colours lost their saturation, slowly drained away to leave nothing but grey, cloudy images. As if a veil of rain separated me from the future. This unreal garden from which I write to you is all the future I now have.

Ayub loved Joséphine and she loved him back. It was an open secret in the village. Rumour had it that Joséphine was a witch. The heir to the palace on the higher hill falling in love with the witch from the valley – that didn't happen every day. But more than anything else, Joséphine was my friend. My second friend, actually, after Ayub. Not to mention that she brought me into the world. Yes, really, the witch, I'm not kidding.

Right, that's where I was going with this, the beginning, the opening scene. So, I was born in a bit of a sluggish year. I've been told that it was a sweaty, muggy summer night, and my poor mother must have been sweaty and muggy, too, I can't even imagine what it's like to be pregnant and sweaty and muggy on such a stifling night. All the roads were closed because of a military curfew, as if the world had schemed to keep me from being born. Maybe there was a thunderstorm. Under such circumstances, there was no chance of getting to a hospital. The closest one was in Nablus, which at that hour and in that weather would take two hours to get to. An isolated palace on the higher hill... some idea that was. But my poor mother didn't panic. She wasn't really the sort to. My father, though? Definitely.

To calm him down, my poor mother suggested calling the neighbour at the bottom of the hill.

"Absolutely not! Are you crazy? She'll cast a spell on us!"

My mother wouldn't have minded having a spell cast on her, though, some sort of magic epidural, or anaesthesia by enchantment, but if she'd said that, my father would have had a coronary.

There were uncles in every corner of the house. Every one of them just as speechless and gutless as my father. All the while, the women were running this way and that – Jeannette gave the marching orders. Imagine that: the men huddled in the shadows, and the women... wait, let me just say this now, for later: I feel like it's when you discover fear, real fear, that you become a real man.

So the men were scared witless, my poor mother was as sweaty as the night, shrieking, half because she actually did hurt and half to convince my father to call this neighbour. So he gave in and sent Ayub to her place.

Ayub was young and I suspect there was already a gleaming darkness in his eyes. He came back, shivering, with the neighbour in question. Her hair was dripping and her clothes – black on black, the colour of Ayub's gleaming darkness – were soaked through. Meaning that my father just got even more panicked and the men huddled in the shadows started shaking with fear and excitement, all while Ayub got to relish being a real man. My mother saw the witch, at which point –

A few hours later, I was born. The roads were still closed, Ayub was now a man in full, my father cradled me in his arms, and my poor mother was dead. My father followed in her footsteps two years later, of that coronary my mother hadn't wanted to risk the night I was born. The witch, though, pulled through, and so did I. She was the one to name me. It happened at the moment that I've just skipped over, when she saw my mother, she told her that I'd been born between day and night, on time's edge, and that I'd come to know, at the very least, how to tell good from bad: a gift that wasn't granted to just anyone. She saw that my mother was about to die, so she told her not to worry. She didn't promise her anything, she simply reassured her. And she offered up to my poor mother, my sweaty mother who was now dying, the name, the admittedly somewhat pompous name, that she would give me: Faysal.

In the garden, Nawal let nature run riot. As for the half-wrecked greenhouse, out of its ruins grew plants as menacing as predators. The broken structure could only just be made out through the creepers that had overrun it. On the day after my return, I went looking for the medlar tree. I had naive hopes that its fruit would dredge up the few happy memories I had of my childhood where, at this very table, not even having bothered to peel them, I had wolfed them down, and, more than once, nearly choked on their pips.

And then I remembered that the prettiest medlar trees were at Joséphine's. I walked to the edge of the lawn, which ended right where the hill drops off into the void, and I looked down. Nothing was left: by the looks of that charred, yellowing plot, one could be excused for believing that the bottom of the valley had always been a wasteland. Wadi al-Arwah. The valley of spirits: it's certainly truer now than ever before. Had I had more courage, I might have gone down to see if some memory of the past remained. Who knows what spirit could be shut away there, could even be angry with me. The valley of Joséphine, my friend, who was known as the witch.

Her magic, if it existed, was of the domestic sort. She knew how to concoct a powder from ants that, if used correctly for a full month, was guaranteed to remove hair permanently; it was popular with the village women. Jeannette had some, in fact. One time, I'd sneaked into her bathroom and rubbed a little of that cream on my cheek. A mistake I regretted immediately: like some divine punishment, a horrific red mark appeared in a line from my temples to my neck.

For three weeks, whenever Joséphine saw me coming, my cheek red and swollen, she would give me a conspiratorial smile. "It'll go away," she reassured me at some point. Then: "You know I can show you all the lotions I have at home," and then, teasingly, she added: "and show you how to use them right."

Joséphine could read coffee grounds and, sometimes, decipher the stars, but only if they were comforting. I knew every nook and cranny of her house by heart. It was an architectural oddity: a small dome covered in greenery. Straight through the front door was the sitting room, which, with its low, rounded ceiling, gave the strange impression of being inside a full belly. The room was wallpapered in green and pink, a child's drawing. But Joséphine's home, really, was her garden. That was her most incredible bit of magic: no matter the season or weather, a motley range of flowers would be in bloom. In front of the house, the oleander was ringed with marvel-of-Peru and rhododendron, concentric circles of clashing roses. Just past that were beds of periwinkle leading to Joséphine's various vegetable patches. By the door, tight clusters of daisy seemed to dance, welcoming in visitors. And yet I had only ever stepped through the doorway at Joséphine's express invitation. The path from the edge of her realm to the door of her house was lined with thistle and knapweed. But what always aroused admiration and jealousy was her stand of black iris – sometimes garnet, most often coal-black – that guarded the entrance to Wadi al-Arwah.

A delicate, childlike charm emanated from this haphazardly tended garden. Passers-by always marvelled at the sight of such clashing flowers crammed together: a riot of colourful, brash fantasies of Joséphine's. All sorts of odd things were whispered about Joséphine. The village children said that she used to be called Joseph but that Joseph had lost her genitals in an unfortunate hunting accident and returned to the village as Joséphine. And this sad accident had given her those magic powers. Everyone regarded Joséphine with fear and awe alike.

When I was young, I thought of Joséphine as a chimera: the word "hermaphrodite", which I only half understood, somehow applied to her. An image that stuck in my head on those rare nights when she and Ayub would spend time together in the sitting room while I went outside to see the fireflies flicker among the flowers.

Jeannette, Ayub, and the cold shadows were yelling in the kitchen.

"You've lost your head," they kept saying, which Ayub did seem to have. He stood, shouted, spluttered.

Jeannette grabbed a Virgin Mary statuette in her hands and said, "Blessed Mother, you've lost your head."

"Try and stop me." Ayub's tone was petulant, as if he were a child and they grown-ups.

"The country's full of women, go to Jerusalem, you can't shake a stick without hitting ten," Jeannette spat out.

Was she jealous?

One of the cold shadows said, to smooth things over, "Well, Ayub, she has a point there."

And now they were yelling so loudly that I couldn't understand them but each yell was like another stab into my belly. Cutting me apart.

The bickering would subside, only to worsen again.

I was in a corner. I had nothing to do with this whole saga, but I still felt like they were all looking at me, never mind that they'd probably forgotten about me.

Jeannette had set the Virgin Mary back on the table. She yelled, "And you! You brought home that... that... slut." She crossed herself and brought her first two fingers to her lips, then to the Virgin Mary.

Ayub grabbed the statuette. "Screw your Virgin Mary."

He threw it as far as he could and the porcelain shattered across the floor.

Everyone fell silent.

*

I went to Joséphine's every afternoon with Ayub. Sometimes, I'd draw her. A pleated dress, as green as the woods, eyes almost the size of her face, very dark hair. I'd draw Ayub too, with big, very dark eyes. Joséphine was the prettiest woman I'd seen in my life and Ayub the handsomest man. He called her Joz and she called him Ass.

Whenever I left the house, I picked a few almonds that I put into a bag one by one, and I brought them to Joséphine as a present.

*

I wasn't usually at Joséphine's when her clients came. Today, though, one of them showed up unexpectedly. She had big sunglasses and very long hair.

She said, "Joséphine, might you be free for a manicure?"

Joséphine said, "Yes yes of course, do you not want the boy here?" The boy being me.

"No, that's all right." She waved her hand as if to swat away some flies, and sat in a pink chair while Joséphine went to get her tools.

"Faysal, go to the well and fetch some water."

When I got back, Joséphine was on a stool and busy

tending carefully to the hands of the lady, who hadn't taken off her sunglasses. The woman said, "But nobody will believe me, Joséphine."

"Oh they will they will," Joséphine replied. "I'm sure of it."

I poured the water into the plastic basin, then sat down and leaned against Joséphine's stool.

"But what about your family, can't you go stay with them?"

The lady was quiet. Then she said, "My family's up north, I don't have a permit to go see them. Besides..."

"Besides what?"

"Besides, my father..."

Joséphine said, "I understand."

But I didn't understand. "Besides, your father what?"

"Faysal!" Joséphine's tone was sharp. "Let us talk." She was very focused on the fingernails. She held a paintbrush; the nails were her canvas.

The lady said, "Oh, Joséphine, Joséphine, what will I do?"

Joséphine stopped and squeezed her hand. "You can stay here."

"But he'll find me. I should go back home."

Joséphine told her to stay but the lady kept saying "No, no" and then "Joséphine, what will I do?" and then "No, no" again. All the while, Joséphine was thoroughly fixated on her hands. She toiled away in silence, and the woman stopped talking. Joséphine was practically glowing. A pastel-toned aura filled the house. It was very reassuring.

Once she was done, Joséphine said, one last time, "Stay here," but the lady said, "I'll be all right, thank you." She didn't wait for her nails to dry. She thanked Joséphine, a very heartfelt thanks. "May the Lord protect you, Joséphine." And she left.

*

Ayub took me to Joséphine's. Today, he was taking his time. He held my hand tight. He knew I usually ran all the way down. I didn't like holding his hand because I wasn't a child. He stopped on the path in front of the Virgin Mary.

"Do you want to see a secret?"

"Always!"

He leaned down and stuck his head in the alcove, behind the Virgin Mary. "There it is! Still all in one piece, can you believe it?" He was holding a red vase. "This was my father's vase. Not bad, huh? It's been there for years. Everyone must have forgotten about it. I only just remembered it this morning. I thought it couldn't be there any more – or if it was, it'd be broken. But see, it's perfect!"

The vase looked pretty but evil. I touched it. It almost seemed to make a noise.

"Odd, isn't it? We should bring it to Joséphine's house and show her."

"No, no," I said, "let's put it back where it belongs." I didn't say: "This vase will ruin the one place that's safe."

"Oh, don't be such a killjoy. Next time, then."

He set the vase where it had been, deep behind the Virgin Mary, and I crossed my fingers that the earth would swallow it up.

*

I sat at Old Jihad's restaurant, waiting for Joséphine and Ayub. They were late. Old Jihad was in a very good mood, just chatting away. Fat Amjad and his fat wife were there.

He was saying to them, "Let's behave ourselves here, Jihad's is a respectable establishment."

"Respectable, my eye!" Fat Amjad chuckled. "People all the way in Amman know this is where you come to eat yourself sick!"

His wife giggled. "And your lamb chops are the talk of Tunis!"

"Tunis! Well, that's really something." Old Jihad stroked his moustache. "You do know you're sitting at the very table where Abu Ammar himself came to try the very best liver in all Palestine? He kissed my cheeks, he blessed me, 'May the Lord always smile on those hands of yours, Jihad.'"

"You ought to have put poison in that liver," Fat Amjad guffawed. "Let him eat himself dead!"

I touched down in a country in Europe and I never came back. What was there to do here? Everyone was dead. I was the lucky and sole heir to all my aunts' and uncles' property. Of plots scattered all across Palestine that I wasted no time selling off. As for the palace, I hired the lawyer from a nearby town; his job was to call me every year and say, "All is well, Mister Faysal, nobody's squatting in the palace, have a wonderful year, may God protect you." Poor guy, every year he had to plop on his fedora and trundle over in his teensy car to check that there was nobody here. I can just see him straining to get the front door open. It'd let out a colossal groan, an absolutely thundering racket. He'd cross himself once before tiptoeing into the half-darkness. He'd inspect the premises as quickly as he could, snap a few shots, keep reciting his prayers to himself – he'd be scared stiff. He could even have come face to face with Nawal, if she'd been so inclined.

On his way back, he'd call me: "No squatters! Happy new year! Talk more soon!"

Honestly, though, who'd be crazy enough to squat in Jabalayn?

With all the cash from those plots (but who were those souls stupid enough to buy up land in the West Bank? I almost feel like I've pulled a fast one on those halfwits: the Armed Forces seized it all after), I've made a very comfortable life for myself in your country.

Nawal summons me every evening to walk through the house and make sure all the lights are off. Back when we heard bombing, we turned on the lights so they'd know there was someone home. Now, we turn them off, so they'll be scared. We turn the lights on for them and turn the lights off for them.

But I'm getting ahead of myself, hold on, I should go back a bit. Where was I? Oh, right, my arrival. When I came into the village, it hadn't changed one bit, as if time had frozen. The flow was stemmed, the rivers stilled, the flowers stunted, the air itself stopped in an eternal moment. The houses' immense stones gleamed white with the winter sun. The walls, even when cracked, were petrified, snared in a springtime I had never seen, in unfathomable seasons. As we made our way past Joséphine's domain, now a desert, I asked the cab driver to stop.

"Are you going to the haunted house up there?" he'd asked; he looked vaguely like an Old Jihad missing his teeth.

"Yes, that's my family home."

In his shock, he whispered, "God protect us," and crossed himself.

I pulled the funeral announcement from my bag: did I have the day and place wrong? Did I just dream up Rita? But it was there, in front of my eyes, in black ink: the vigil for Tante Rita was this Sunday. The sun was already starting to set. I wavered, then resolved to get out of the car there so I could get to the house on the hill, right there, by foot. Having made my way from the road, I tackled the footpath that laboriously wound around the hill. It had been thought up and planned out as a stroll: as they ascended, guests would gradually discover Palestine's landscape unfurling before their eyes. On the side of the hill, by the path, Ibrahim had had an altar built, and I stopped at it, out of breath. An alcove had been cut into the rock and inside stood a marble statue of the Virgin Mary, hands outstretched in prayer. Behind her was a starry sky of ultramarine earthenware tiles, shot through with small bursts of saffron. Around the alcove, tall pines stood sentry like warrior protectors of the Virgin Mary. Jeannette used to say that Ibrahim was especially devoted to Mariam. The woods – so we called the fig and pear and apple and almond and pine trees further down the hill – were untouched, virginal, antediluvian. The light receded and the evening's colours slowly submerged the hill and the village. As I had nearly reached the mountain's peak, I glanced back and took in the village over my shoulder: it struck me as positively oceanic.

At the top of the hill, the bougainvillea awaited me. It stood higher than I remembered. Monstrous, even: its flowers had crept up to the third-storey windows, which they were close to engulfing. From the outside, the house looked like a pink island. Hardly a pretty sight – on the contrary, it was somewhat obscene. Confronted with this monstrosity, I felt fear and wavered at the door. "But I'm home,"

I reminded myself, "and this place belongs to me. I'm not an intruder. I can go in." I turned back to the bougainvillea. "Yes, I'm home," I told it. "I don't belong to this place; it belongs to me. Ayub and Joséphine saw each other for the last time under this bougainvillea. I watched over their final meeting. I stood guard. I'm home. I deserve to be here."

I opened the door. The house was clean inside. Everything as it should be. Nothing had collapsed, not a single spiderweb, no scorpion's nest, as I'd imagined. Nothing had moved. Had the lawyer hired a cleaning crew every year? But that wasn't his job and I'd have noticed it on the typed invoices that he sent me each year with a polite little note attached. I was alone in the house. No vigil, no long line of mourners come to offer their condolences, nothing.

The house was upset that I'd left. It twitched. It didn't welcome me. I suppose I had been envisioning a prodigal son's return. But nobody ever waits for prodigal sons with open arms; they curse them, insult them; a mechanical, coalfired rage stokes spite in the hearts of those forsaken. I hadn't forsaken anyone, though. I felt chilly and a bit scared. I sat down on the first sofa I happened upon, hoping to take refuge in its soft red folds. Who could be upset with me? And what made me decide to come back here? The light filtering through the half-closed shutters cast ghostly shadows on the floor, worrisome vapours that silently observed me.

From every corner, eyes stared at me. Each object in this house looked at me with bitterness, daring me to take just one step further. The Dresden figurines smiled at me malevolently. The chandeliers whistled their hatred. The yawning sofas bared their teeth.

Everything was tidy and threatening: none of the creatures I expected to find here – snakes, rats, vermin, pests. As if the house were still inhabited. I felt like an intruder, under the irreproachable gaze of all these objects that, unlike me, had remained here.

Instinctively, I took refuge in my childhood bedroom. Ayub had slept there when he was little and, reportedly, so had his own father Ibrahim as a child. It hadn't changed, it had stayed exactly as it was the day I left. As if I'd left for school this very morning. Was I nine years old? I looked in the mirror to make sure. No, I was the right age. My eyes were dark-rimmed from the trek, my face dirty.

Why did I feel like an impostor here? "I'm in my home," I kept repeating out loud, then, for anyone who might be listening: "This house, this hill, are mine. Mine alone. I have the papers in my luggage to prove that this belongs to me from top to bottom, all the way to the main road." In the drawing room adjacent to the kitchen, bouquets of white flowers had been set on each table. All of a sudden, the exhaustion of the trip came over me. Sleep. It was already late. Before heading back to my room, I unthinkingly walked through what I called "the real house", the one behind all the drawing rooms, behind all the spaces built for others. Here, we were in inscrutable tradition. A simple sitting room, chairs with plastic slipcovers, a tiny kitchen with a bisque-hued fridge, and three bedrooms. Mine, then Jeannette's, then Ayub's. The others – the cold shadows – lived in the rest of the house, on continents I barely knew.

My bed was made: soft pillows that smelled of eucalyptus, immaculately white sheets and quilts. Not the least trace of damp or mould. The mattress felt like new. I let out a contented sigh as I lay down. With my eyes on the ceiling, it occurred to me that the house was ready for a wedding. I sank into a deep-rooted feeling of trust. Under other circumstances, I might have run screaming out of the place. Or I might have shut myself in my bedroom to watch the whole night for invaders. But this trust, so soft and warm, had filled me to the brim, and I fell asleep with particular pleasure.

"No, I don't want to go back up." I'd spoken calmly.

I stood at the door as Ayub said, "Come on, we need to get back in time for dinner."

"No. I want to stay here, I want to sleep here. It's the holidays. Tell them up there. You're my uncle, if I stay with you, they won't worry."

Ayub said, "You're going to make things difficult for me."

"No, no, I won't, I'm staying and sleeping here. You're going to take me up, and then you're going to come back down, it's not fair."

"Another time, I promise," Ayub said. "We'll tell them first."

"No, there won't be another time. I want to sleep here tonight." I wouldn't be told no. I stood my ground. Ayub looked at me and I looked at him and scrunched my brows. I'd won. Ayub sighed.

"I'll let them know," he said to Joséphine.

Joséphine let out a chuckle. She rubbed my head and said, "You're a little old wahsh, you know that? A fierce thing. Like me, like Ayub. We're a gang aren't we!"

That night, I fell asleep between Ayub and Joséphine. Ayub grumbled but I knew he was happy.

*

"And Moshe Dayan, yes, Moshe Dayan himself came!" Old Jihad was boasting to Ayub and Joséphine. Never mind that it was nothing to boast about. "That was way back when. And of course he loved it, too. He could have dined at any of Tel Aviv's best restaurants, and he said, he said, 'Jihad, you're really some chef.'"

Even I knew who Moshe Dayan was. He was a terrifying man with an eyepatch like a classic Hollywood baddie; just his face meant trouble for us all.

"Ha!" Ayub was bent over laughing. "You should have poisoned him, too. Who else's been to your restaurant?"

Old Jihad said, "Everyone, everyone's been. And they all loved it."

And Joséphine piped up, "I'm starting to think that if Jihad could be talked into poisoning just half his guests Palestine would be so, so much better off."

*

I'd done something stupid. I was seven. I came back from school, straight to the house. I didn't stop at Old Jihad's to spend a few minutes imagining blasting off from here, far from the cold shadows. No chance of rushing down to Joséphine's. In any case, Ayub was on the higher hill with the others.

I'd done something really stupid.

The house's stones had an icy chill.

"Go to your room."

I spied on them through the keyhole. The cold shadows

had gathered around the old stove. Jeannette was warming her wrinkly hands.

"I just don't believe it. He has to be punished."

Jeannette suggested the belt.

Voices overlapped; Ayub said, "Are you mad? Of course not! He has to be told what he did wrong. He's got too much imagination, that's all."

"Insisting that we talk to ghosts!" It bothered Jeannette no end that I hadn't been given a thorough religious schooling.

"Do you really think," one of the cold shadows was asking, "that, once he's gotten the belt, he'll start believing in God?"

Everyone laughed; I shuddered. How cruel it was for them to laugh like that when I, the condemned soul, was waiting for them to decide my punishment.

"Back in my day, they got the ruler," Jeannette hissed.

"Have you lost your mind, Jeannette? Absolutely not. What planet are you on?" That was Ayub talking.

Jeannette's eyes were fixed on him. "This is all your fault, you know. Nobody says a thing here, everybody turns a blind eye, but what he said, it's what he saw in Wadi al-Arwah when you were busy with your—"

I didn't hear the word she used because Ayub was already standing up and shouting at Jeannette, "Don't you even start!"

And Jeannette said that it was the talk of the whole village. My family was Ayub and Joséphine and Old Jihad. But

Jeannette was the oldest, so we had to listen to her. With her tortoiseshell glasses, she looked like a dragon. Ayub would do it, and with his belt: those were her orders.

I covered my eyes.

Ayub was standing. Ayub had black hair and a pale face. Ayub had deep, sad, wild eyes and lashes just as long as any falsies that the village girls might put on.

He said, "Come here." He didn't look at me.

I examined the gleaming darkness of his eyes. He had me lie across his lap. I could feel his crotch. I gathered my thoughts. I escaped into my head, took refuge in my mind. They couldn't reach me there. What if they heard me? When my thoughts got too noisy, I was sure everyone could hear the racket they made. Maybe even see them. I hid away. His hand came down with a loud slap once, again, a third time. A crack that filled my ears and jolted my head. A scorching fire across my bottom. He got up. He took off his belt. The sound of a belt being undone: that was where it always started.

"Don't move," Jeannette ordered. I wanted to scowl at her.

Ayub thundered, "Son of a bitch!" but I forgave him. I knew why he was insulting me. He'd never spanked anyone. Of course he was going through the same motions as his own father in the old days when men were barbarians. Ayub called me an ass and in my head I thanked him, because I knew that each insult was a message for me: "I'm sorry, I don't know how to get you out of this." That was a fateful moment. A secret kept between the two of us.

Jeannette said, "What you did was unacceptable. Do you understand that?"

"Yes, yes, Tante, I understand." But no sooner had I formulated that response in my head than the belt had cracked in the air and across my rear. It came down so hard that it had me burning all over. I forgot the secret pact that Ayub and I had sealed, I forgot Tante Jeannette and all the others. The pain rushed through my whole body all the way to my eyes, which burst into tears. And in that pain, I wished, from the bottom of my heart, that Ayub would die, that he would fall on the ground and twitch. That he would choke, that he would hurt so much that he couldn't speak, that he would plead with me and I would look on and that would be his punishment.

The sun was rising. I woke up, sprawled across the cold tiles of my bedroom floor. I tried to hide deep in the woods of my mind. I had no idea what lay on the other side of my door.

I'd have liked to say that, in the gardens, as I took in the hill's singular scent, I saw once more a potential grandmother, a wild woman, seated on the terrace and telling me of wonders, regaling me with tales of mermaids in the rivers and jinns hidden in the bushes. That I remembered once more afternoons with Joséphine taking me by the hand to walk through the landscape. I'd have liked to be able to tell you that, with this unforeseen return, I had regained this part of myself. That as I plumbed the house I rediscovered both its scents and my sense of touch, I regained my sense of hearing and, at last, my ability to listen the way I had before darkness had spread wide its wings. But that would have been a lie.

I made my way to the kitchen. A freshly cooked breakfast awaited me. I asked out loud, "Who's there?" Nobody in the kitchen, nobody in the drawing room. I had the vague thought that someone might be trying to poison me, but I was hungry enough that I took my chances; the fried eggs quivered on the plate, the bread was fresh. The tomatoes and garlic, the labneh and za'atar, set out in small ceramic bowls, were irresistible bursts of white, red, and green. I dug in with the appetite of a child just home from school.

What did I do for the rest of the day? I don't know, I explored the house under the unwavering eye of whoever had cooked for me. In the evening, a dinner was waiting for me, mountains of rice swimming in a goat's-cheese sauce upon which massive chunks of lamb had pride of place. There was enough to feed a dozen at the very least.

As I ate, I thought I could see something like two eyes watching me from the kitchen. I was sure I was hallucinating; I'd have to leave the next day.

Then I noticed that the eyes were like the ones I could never forget, Ayub's eyes. "Is that you?" I thought. I didn't dare to open my mouth. "Is that you, Uncle? Talk to me if you want, I'm here, I'm home again, I'll stay here, right here, for all time, just for you, if you want. Talk to me." The eyes watched me, but did not move.

So I decided to have a shower, and wait for those eyes to finally emerge from their silence. That the shower was new, that it worked, that there was water (*hot* water!) all struck me as even more inconceivable than the food. And the eyes were there, looking away, clearly for modesty's sake. "Ayub, you can look." If only he knew! In the massive pink-tiled bathroom, Ibrahim had put in stained-glass windows in vibrant hues – magenta, chartreuse, goldenrod – depicting tropical birds in a jungle. Parrots and toucans filtered the intense iridescent light bathing the room in a rainbow halo. I looked at myself in the mirror, clean at last, the jungle behind me, and in the shower's mist, two eyes staring at me.

"Well, Uncle, am I being spied on? Come here, Ayub, talk to me, please."

But the eyes did not talk. Instead, I heard whispering from the bowels of hell, wiswiswis coming from every corner of the house. A dull, low sound, voices that pleaded and begged, others that laughed, voices that didn't try to tell me anything, only to alert me to their presence.

I didn't write to my office to let them know I wasn't coming in. I didn't write to you. I didn't write to anyone. I spent the rest of the day as I did all the ones after: going through the house from top to bottom. I had made up my mind to leave again, but I couldn't tear myself away from this place so quickly. I knew that when I did leave, it would be for good. If nothing else, I had to say all my goodbyes properly. Last time, I hadn't had the chance to.

I woke up. It was the second morning. I felt full of a peculiar energy. I wasn't afraid of what might lie on the other side of the door. I was home. Today I'd call up a few acquaintances here, I'd find someone to come and help me put the house up for sale; I'd never really managed to get my head around real-estate jargon in this land – words with odd, somewhat Ottoman sounds like tabo and sumsar – and I'd never be able to pull it off. "I'll deal with that today," I thought, "and then I'll leave. Simple as that."

Breakfast was waiting for me, outside this time, under the almond trees. A table had been set up, the same one you would eventually bring out for us to dine at in a sea of fireflies, and the same tablecloth, embroidered with blue. As if I had been invited to a romantic dinner – me, myself, and I across from the world. The sky was shot through with pastel hues; it was doing its best, one might have thought, to mask its malevolence. The eyes were waiting for me. I wanted to say: "Good morning, Ayub. I've missed you so much. For twenty-five years, my life's been meaningless without you. Good morning, good morning, Ayub, how beautiful your eyes are, how I wish I could touch them, how I wish I could jump into your arms, even if you never, not once in your life, would have let me. Death's made a softie of you."

I ate slowly, and drank the piping-hot coffee. Then I ventured a "Salam alaikum".

I don't know if she appeared all of a sudden, in the blink of an eye, or if her smile had come first, a prelude to her eyebrows, and then to her nose, her face, her whole body. She materialised, there, full-fleshed and real, breathing, and she wasn't Ayub. Her features first, then, as if an invisible hand were colouring her in, her skin, her clothes, gradually this figure's contours took shape. A multicoloured mist that watched me with curiosity and examined every feature of my face. She was wearing a grey jacket with thin blue stripes. Then, after several minutes, she gave me a familiar smile. "I've been waiting for you! Welcome, welcome." She got up and she took flesh. She was no mist but a proper lady full of concern, a woman who would be called "my aunt".

"Would you like some more coffee? How did you like my breakfast? And dinner last night, that mansaf? That was for you, you and you alone!" She drew close to my face. She had no smell. She exhaled no breath from her mouth. "Ah, yes, the spitting image of your grandfather! I've always said so, always."

I thought of Ayub, I didn't know who this woman was, this *thing*, I had no idea what to say. She looked at me, as if waiting for my reply.

"Did you like your bedroom? You did see, didn't you, it's just like when you were little. Nothing changed. I took care of every last thing. After all this time, you see, after all those souls... left, I realised that was my job."

I did recognise those features. I could make out, in her bourgeois smile, something of Ayub, something of myself.

She got up and rushed into the house. She came back with a plate on which two tall glasses and two bottles were clinking. "A vodka soda for the reunion?"

Then I spoke for the first time since she had appeared: "It's a bit early for that, isn't it?"

She let out a gentle laugh. "Ah, *that* got you talking! Alcoholism does run in the family, it's a real problem... Well, for me, that's what's made me solid!" She poured two glasses for us all the same, and filled them to the brim. We clinked glasses, at which point I was sure I recognised her. Had I actually seen this woman before, had I actually known her?

"For forty years now, I've been the caretaker of this property." She ran her finger along one of the chairs set up in the garden. "I make sure to dust the house every morning; I wash the windows every week." She paused. "You did see how clean they are? And I tend the garden as well." She thought for a moment. "On my own, I do the work that, back in my time, was done by a dozen maids. Nothing's moved, not a single object, and everything's clean. And I've been waiting for you: the palace will die. You need to come back, you need to settle here. To bring the village back to life! Yes, I feel alone here. A little; I do talk to Ibrahim up there. He was never so understanding before his death. But, you know, I was thinking of you all along. Have you ever experienced this lovely feeling of knowing that, no matter what, there's someone in some faraway land who's thinking of us? It's a thought, a thread that always connected me to you and when I was really too lonely or feeling scared, I would think:

'Faysal, wherever he is, will come back. If he doesn't come back, Faysal, wherever he is, will at least be thinking of this place.'"

Me? She was thinking about me? And as if she could read my thoughts, she went on: "Of course! That's why I summoned you back here. Come, smell the narcissus and the jasmine over there. This is your world; this is your destiny. I've preserved it all for you."

"I didn't dare appear in front of you." She inhaled the garden's scents with theatrical pleasure and, with a glance at the almond trees, said: "It's hard to describe these trees, isn't it?"

I wasn't sure how to respond, let alone react to this thing, this ghost, I suppose, even now I'm not sure what exactly she is, assuming I haven't made her up. Yes, it's hard to describe almond blossoms, "not snow and not cotton", I'd read the poem, too, I'd caught the echo, I didn't need the same old song.

I recognised Nawal – my grandmother, that's her name – as I flipped through the photo albums. Imm Ayub to everyone else, Nawal to me. Possibly a figment of my weary brain.

"Is this how one tends one's home: leaving it to moulder under the weight of years without returning every so often to make sure that the power still works, that there's been no water damage, that the stones are still like new? Only now do you come back, having sold off all the rest, having bled dry all that generations upon generations had killed themselves to build and accumulate. You sold it all and left this house open to attack from all directions – all so you can live like a carefree little pasha out there. Three generations' hard work gone up in smoke just to make mister happy.

"And all the while, as you were having your fun over there doing Lord knows what, who was supposed to take care of the house here? Who was supposed to make sure that nothing went to pieces? Who was supposed to ward off mice and cockroaches, clean the curtains, turn over the mattresses, scare off settlers and squatters? Well, little pasha? Shame on your blood! They built you a palace on the higher hill only for you to leave it to rack and ruin, on a whim...

"You'll have to forgive me, it's my loneliness talking, my sadness. I do miss Ibrahim. I'd hoped to find him again here. Really, with all my heart, I did. But he isn't here. Nobody came back. There's only me. Lord knows why. I don't mean to heap reproaches on you like that; it's because I've been here on my own for so long. I waited for them to come back but they never did. So I hoped that, one day, you might take over. Might relieve me of my obligations for just ten minutes. To see you and smile at you. I waited and waited; the settlers started closing in more and more often. You can imagine what I've been reduced to, ghostly sleights of hand, making a few doors screech and shaking some chains. The chains we used for lamb sacrifices! Sometimes I yanked on the tails of cats that chose to take up residence here so they would screech and dash out between the settlers' paws. I don't lack imagination. Their visits became more and more frequent: just last week, ten of them showed up. Six clumsy men, gorillas, and four gangly teenagers, no more than kids. They rummaged through the house, oh so fastidious like the soldiers and policemen they are. They didn't steal anything, none of it interested them, I think. You end up thinking: it's too sophisticated for them here, whatever would they come to steal? The fabrics, the silver, the china, they wouldn't understand any of it. There was a ringleader, of course, a man with a suspicious-looking head. They all had rifles. How useful that I do understand a little Hebrew. They wanted to make sure that nobody was living here. I panicked. Little ghostly sleights of hand were all well and good when there was only three of them, when they didn't have their wits about them, but I could see the resolve in that fat buffalo's eyes. No ghost would be enough to keep them from settling in here, after all, he was certain that God was on his side. I didn't think of you immediately. At first, I just prayed as hard as I could that Ibrahim might come back, or his father, or Ayub, or Jeannette. I prayed and prayed for Jeannette, she'd have known what to do, she'd have aimed a rifle and scared them off. I stared at the horizon and I prayed, and I told myself that they'd all come back, and together we'd all guard the house.

"One day I heard the sound of a car and I thought, 'Finally! Someone!' I was determined to talk to whoever it was, even if it was your stupid lawyer. But it was a couple. They were in a truck. They stopped in the village. And, just like that, they unloaded their belongings and moved in. Just like that! He was a terribly handsome man wearing a kippah, looking awfully grim with his blonde wife who was very pregnant, and their six kids. I'll say it, they didn't have the least bit of sense. You need a lot of gall or a lot of stupidity to come and move in like this, in a ghost town with no running water or electricity, and with a whole gaggle of kids. I'd be pretty worried about the place being haunted. They have no sense at all, that's how they're winning. I don't know what their plan is. They haven't made their way up here yet. At some point, they'll start thinking, 'Isn't that a nice house up there on the hill?' and they'll come to set one of their kids up there. Or maybe it's the man with a suspicious-looking head who'll be coming back."

She came in and out of focus as she spoke, as if some antenna had a bad signal. I get the impression that her existence here depends on her feelings. Her contours grew jumbled when she was annoyed, and settled again when she was at ease; her complexion deepened as she shrieked, and returned to some degree of grey as her fury subsided. Even her voice was by turns staticky and clear throughout the day. But no matter her state, it was clear she was family. I could tell that we shared, or had once shared, the same mediocre blood.

What did I have to say to her? I hadn't asked for any of this: not this war, not the one before, not the one after. Our whole family's story, at heart, was one of uselessness. All who had preceded me had been utterly, irremediably useless. They'd left by way of inheritance both this house (palace, my arse) and their uselessness. They'd lost everything, absolutely everything: their wars, their battles, their homes, even their courage. As for me, I'd resigned myself to my uselessness. Like the rest of them, I had no expectation that an angel might appear to us one day and tell us: "You were right! Sorry, our mistake. We'll fix it." Our whole history was one long string of catastrophes and I certainly wasn't about to get myself into another one on this old lady's orders. If it was anyone's fault that we had ended up here, it was the fault of people like her who'd sold their dreams, then their weapons, then their children. The lady revolutionary now the lady patron of arts. And she actually thought she could hold on to this house for... a few days? A few months? However long it took for us to be snuffed out?

For the first few days, Nawal talked nonstop from when I left my bedroom until I returned to go to sleep. She had decades of stories and complaints to share. She was full to the brim, bursting with words. But why? She ought to have done something sooner, maybe when she was hosting those dinners and parties. I'd walked away from it all.

I'd walked away from it all... yes, I, the offspring of businessmen and high-society ladies, resistance fighters when they could respectably be so, I'd walked away from it all. So what if we disappeared, we rifle and underwear sellers? Underwear sellers... is that what I don't dare to confess to you? It's so stupid, it's nothing to do with me, but I still feel ashamed... So what if we disappeared? We wouldn't be the first or the last to. My greatest fear isn't being annihilated. It's being misunderstood.

"We're not in some western, Imm Ayub," I'd snapped at her the first time she tried to tell me that I had a battle to fight.

"Maybe you aren't, but *they* are. You should have seen them! Real cowboys. Thugs. Would you really leave our house at the mercy of thugs?"

At the airport, I was half dozing on the moving walkway when a simple, understated poster stretching for several metres alongside me caught my attention: COMING SOON TO HAIFA, A MONUMENTAL LABOUR OF MEMORY: THE MUSEUM OF PALESTINIAN CULTURE. And in that moment, I understood it was over, that underwear and rifle sellers were a thing of the past. If they memorialise us, it's because they've won; because, with this pre-emptive act of memorialisation, they've already overseen our annihilation. The feeling that the moving walkway was bearing me toward catastrophe. It used to be that we were accused of being fictional. They would stand up in their parliament buildings and stare at foreigners and say, "No, these are fictional beings! They do not exist! They never existed! They are murdering us and they are dangerous and they never existed!" Now they are building a museum, now they are placing us behind glass alongside some embroidered dresses and an olive press. They wave a wand and poof: we are now truly the stuff of fiction.

Which is how I know I won't be swayed by Nawal's rants: the family line ends with me. After Faysal, snip: the vasectomy of a whole dynasty. No offspring to carry a family's name, a nation's regret, a father's moniker. No thanks. I'm a lizard stranded on an island lost in the universe and that suits me just fine.

"Can you even say you know this country's soul, its murmur? Behold the light outside, how perfect it is; behold the horizon in the distance as it dances and laughs, draws nearer then further away like a child, playing by the water. My land is fire my land is ocean my land is a hymn winding through the hills, a hum fading, vanishing in the din. Behold the mineral spring and the thunder and, down there, see the foxglove covering Old Jihad, there where the world ends. Would you leave such a gem, a pearl, in the hands of barbarians? Do you understand, little one, little idiot, that here is where all will be decided? Leave, and you will be nothing any more. Leave, and you will lose yourself. Would you choose not to hear Jerusalem, its dull roar, down there, and, closer, not to hear the song of hundreds of villages? Did I beget forsakers, who have snuffed out, succumbed to minor disasters? I who almost took up arms, I who would, today, if I could, take a kitchen knife and go down the hill to slit the throat of every single soul I saw... I can see him, there, in your eyes. You're like him, too fond of the better things in life. You're like him, introspective and self-absorbed. I'm not surprised you all turned out cowards."

Sometimes Nawal can be a hateful creature, a monster. That morning, she came and watched me as I sat in the garden, staring into the void. Her eyes blazed. I was certain she would punish me with a slow, agonising death. She drew near and terror overcame me. I couldn't move a limb. I thought of you. It's true, I'm forgetting you, but sometimes you still come to mind. Like fog, yet still here. Nawal's eyes were an inch from my face and I couldn't move a single muscle and I kept saying, "please, please," and Nawal, in her fury, looked ready to devour me. She stayed silent, face to face with me, for a few seconds, and the wiswiswis came back and swarmed the two of us. I begged, "Nawal, please, please, please." Suddenly, she spun on her heel and disappeared into the house; a gust of wind, as if at her behest, slammed the door shut and shook the house.

But I've already lost the thread. Just the memory of it makes me shiver. Nawal's sitting across from me right now, terrified. She's listening in case they're there. And I recall her in that demonic, vengeful form, so long ago, that form she never again showed me, and I don't know how to reconcile this poor, terrified, depressive ghost with the vengeful spirit I'd beheld.

But it wasn't my plan to tell you about that. I didn't start this so I could tell you about that. I wanted to tell you... yes, when you left. You left, like that, because I didn't hear you and I didn't see you. You were patient. You waited a whole week for me. You stayed in this house, alone, beside me, and you touched me with such care, you stroked me to reassure me, you listened to me when I managed to talk, you tried to bring a bit of the real world into this palace of ghosts and you almost succeeded.

And then you left. What's there to say? A slammed door, a deafening sound, I'd never heard anything like it, you'd left and when the door slammed shut I knew you'd never be back and it was over for me. So I did what anyone in my place would have done, I think, I locked the heavy deadbolt on top and turned the key in the small lock on the bottom. I went out onto the terrace. I looked out at the night already starting to give way to day. I wondered how things could change like that, how without any warning night could become day and how you, George, who only a few hours ago had been kissing me, how you could now be gone forever. I took a deep breath. I looked at the darkness slowly dissipating, evaporating even as out of its depths came the light of day, and I made my decision.

I sat down in a red leather chair in the Jaffa room and, there and then, I dreamed of this land I hate. I started imagining that, this day, the sun would be so strong, so victorious, so pitiless, that it would scorch everything in its path. Each ray would incinerate trees, houses, people, and, at the end of the day, the desert's wind would rise above a land made

97

all the purer, a land without anything. For the first time with-out anything. For the first time, here, there would be silence. A very, very nice land in which to die.

Nawal was waiting for me in the kitchen. She was happy you'd left. She was cooking. She was whistling. I had been calm all this while, but her smugness pushed me over the edge.

"It's your fault! It's your fault he left. Why did you do that? He was the only one, the only one. He actually wanted to find me. I didn't ask anything of him and he still came. Do you want to keep me on a leash here like some dog? He came to find me. Who in your life ever came to find you? He was so patient. And maybe if he'd been patient for just a day or two more, who knows, maybe..."

She listened in silence. She gave a mischievous half-smile, as if she'd done something naughty.

"He could have saved me. I'd have packed my bags. I'd have turned off all the lights. I'd have locked the doors. And I'd have climbed into his car and we'd have headed back and I'd have left you here, all alone, because you're the one who doesn't want to leave."

Nawal wasn't smiling now. Gently, she replied: "You're the one who didn't want to leave with him."

I wanted you to leave. I didn't want you to be patient for just a day or two more. It's a double bind: all I want is to follow you, to go back, to leave behind this house and this ghost and these wretched memories. But I can't bring myself to abandon this strip of land where Joséphine and Ayub are buried, where the corpse of my grandfather Ibrahim is snuggled up in the earth to that of his son Ayub, my love. I want to follow you, but not just yet. One day, when I'm set free, I'll come back. A happier day. When all is gone. For now, I'm handcuffed to this sky and this cemetery.

Second day. No, third. I'm not sure any more. Since Nawal appeared. Alone in the bedroom, I sat on the bed. I thought of you. You'd reappeared. This boy like an elf back there in a land of mist and gold. Your name was already distant but I saw your eyes and I smelled your scent on the bed. See. I took my phone to write to you but on the nightstand there was a photo album that Nawal must have left for me. Under other circumstances, I'd have admired her tenacity, her firm conviction that fate would one day be on our side at last. And that, until then, she'd stop at nothing. She had her back to the wall, so she had her claws out. Of course the Israelis were driving her crazy. How, she seemed to be asking, was she supposed to accept that such boors, such brutes might get the better of her, Nawal? (Never would it have occurred to her that she might owe at least some of this disdain to class hatred. Would she rather that, say, aristocrats be the ones to seize her house?)

As foreign languages became the province of women, so my family became bourgeois. The men – the village Khalils, Habibs, and Hannas – were merchants of the finest kind, and had always been speakers of languages of every stripe, the better to hawk their wares. When I say "speakers", to be clear, that means they knew how to say "high-quality" and "great bargain" in those languages. With the next generation, they added "Christian" to their vocabulary; with the one after, "Holy Land". Three generations later, Khalil was now Charles, Habib had reinvented himself as Aimé, and Hanna was rechristened John, and they all saw themselves as aristocrats. The women had long only spoken, well, I was going to say Arabic, but it wasn't Arabic they spoke, not quite: it was the Jabalayn dialect.

My aunt Jeannette once, in a rare moment of tenderness, showed me, not without some pride, the report that a random Orientalist visiting my village had made in the 1840s. He had mentioned one of my forebears, "an esteemed doctor, tur-jman, & polyglot". A turjman... a proper gentleman who was rather Oriental yet very easy to deal with, who served as guide for European tourists. Hence my family name. I bear the name of my foreignness. And over the years, things were embellished: "We were always ferrymen, bridging the shores of the Mediterranean," Jeannette was fond of saying. But in fact, the forebear in question had to scrape together a bit of extra money by leading tourists to a dark cave nearby, promising them: "Here, miracle, Virgin Mary, authentic!"

The Orientalist highlighted that my forebear was a refined, practically European man. This depended on the little smart-arse making sure the clueless traveller never saw hide nor hair of his wife with heavy features and a huge nose, who didn't speak a word of French or English; even her Arabic had the undertones of the illiterate peasant that she was. A fat peas-ant who worked the fields and cooked the whole day while her husband traipsed around, declaring, "Authentic miracle!" She was not a little proud of being married to the local polyglot, even if she didn't understand much and thought he was kind of a moron when he put on all those airs.

All the women after her were no different: big noses, not much for smiling or talking. I can put my finger on exactly when foreign languages got into these women's lives. It was in Nawal's generation. She and her sisters-in-law were the first women in my family to get a handle on those languages the men had spoken for centuries. And those women's features changed as well. As those formerly hardy, ugly matriarchs grew fluent in French, English, and Italian, their bodies became wispier. Thinner noses and slimmer faces for dances; narrower hips for journeys; lighter skin. That this crabby old lump purporting to be my great-grandmother, the wife of So-and-So, could have been the origin point from which Ibrahim had emerged, took some serious suspension of disbelief. Likewise to imagine that Nawal could have called this shapeless mass "mother-in-law".

Here, compare these two photos, taken thirty years apart. Same background, same setup: a woman spending an afternoon at the Dead Sea. In the first one, a huge peasant, scarf wrapped around her head, standing with her back to the sea. She's staring at the camera with hostility. Not even a hint of a smile – but then again, she isn't smiling in any photos. I wouldn't want to attribute any ill will to this old woman; I can't claim to know the history of smiles in photography. Maybe she was having the time of her life and a good laugh all around but one simply didn't smile in photos back then.

In this shot, she's saying no to the sea's many pleasures, no to the whole premise of the photo.

Now consider the second woman. This one is Nawal. Her black hair's framing her face and accentuating her already slim features. See her nose, how she stands aloof. You can tell the story of an entire family through noses. See how thin this one is, as if it bore no relation to her mother's. Nawal's nose is her way of saying no. Just like that, she's turning her back on her entire lineage. "My nose is European," she's proudly declaring. "I made off with my mother's and grandmothers' cooking, and carried on their rage. The rage that made them clumsy flows right through my body, makes me a flame. They were poor, withered plants; I'm a chrysanthemum from a distant land. Behold my dress, its whiteness as striking as the horizon. It shows off my curves. Light pours into me and exalts me. Those women were fat black heaps that blocked light. I'm its blaze. I smile. I ravish. They are darkness, nameless earth. I am Palestine."

Pure thinness; but our ancestors' blood runs through our veins and our bodies betray us: in the fullness of time, our noses widen and spread across our faces, to restore us to ourselves. Every woman in my family, without exception, has had her nose done.

And I, in turn, have chosen the darkness into which my mothers and grandmothers and great-grandmothers have retreated with their ugly noses and their broken tongues. I've gone into hibernation for them, I guess.

But enough of my digressions. The next day, when I woke up, I stayed in bed a little longer. The whole equinox had begun. Maybe I dreamed up Nawal. A ghost, really... And maybe I never actually went back, maybe I was still in my actual bed, the one in a European country, with George next to me in our square, modern, stainless-steel apartment with bay windows overlooking a city of perpetual light. And then I came back to: no George, just the photo album I'd looked through the night before. So there really was a ghost waiting patiently on the other side of the door to pester me. The smell of coffee came. What kind of ghost cooked breakfast? I kept leafing through the album. Full of photos from the sixties. The dates and places were pencilled in on the back in handwriting so spidery I could barely read it. I recognised Nawal and was astonished that the figure now before me and the figure from the sixties were one and the same. The same curls, the same nose. The same dresses, dark and almost militaristic. The same almond eyes squinting at the world like an enemy. Nawal next to Ibrahim, laughing, in Beirut. Looking lovingly at him in Cairo. On his arm, rigid and aloof, in Nablus. Nawal next to Ibrahim, in Paris, London, Jerusalem, Isfahan, Beirut, Amman, Tunis. Family photos with their children and their parents. Ayub as a child. His big eyes. My mother in Nawal's arms. Ibrahim had a particular, fragile beauty. Something already cracked in his gaze. Ayub looked like him, it's true, but where there was an animal quality to his face, a prickly aspect to his body, Ibrahim, by contrast, seemed translucent. A photo of Ibrahim as a boy at his first communion. He's wearing white trousers and looking at the camera, his chin resting in his upturned right hand. Someone took care to arrange the photos chronologically. For the most part, '69 to '74 must have been a nonstop party. Nawal roaring with laughter, Nawal dancing, Nawal introducing a stranger to another stranger. A face kept showing up at these parties, like a ghostly apparition. A head visible atop a Greek Orthodox monk's habit. A leonine, fierce-looking man. He looked young; in his forties, maybe. He was handsome. He was there, in the shadow or the light, in each photo I noticed from this period: as if he were always the one around whom the balance of light and dark in the photo were organised. I spent a few minutes studying a photo taken in the Jaffa room. They're standing, Nawal on the right, Ibrahim on the left, and this priest in the middle. His profile, ominous and seductive, emerges from the shadows. He's taller than either of them, almost set in relief in his long black cape. Looking at me.

Nawal sat at the table, waiting for me, smoking a cigarette. Well, that was a first. Bathed in daylight, her body seemed solid even if slightly phosphorescent. And I could make out the puffs of smoke being inhaled into her mouth and drawn down to her lungs. So clearly that the smoke looked like a snake trapped in this woman.

"That's bad for your health, you know," I said, teasingly.

She ignored my remark. "Are you planning to stay?"

"I haven't decided."

I was already feeling calmer than yesterday, having resigned myself to the fact that I would be staying here a good while.

"Who's the man in the photos from the album?"

She carefully took a photo with one hand while she stuck the other through the open window to flick her cigarette ash onto the narcissus outside.

She pretended to spit. "Bah! Rasputin."

"Sorry?"

"A priest who visited often after the war. Everyone swooned at his feet, but I was never a fan of him. Rasputin, I called him..."

"Why?"

"Never mind that! Here, look how pretty I used to be. And your grandfather, too. He broke plenty of hearts, you know. He wouldn't look at any woman but me."

She got up and came back out of the kitchen with a plate of fried eggs, za'atar and olive oil, labneh, and medlar. "Eat, eat." She poured herself a glass of vodka, and she watched me attentively.

The way Nawal runs the house inspires admiration. An empty house, yet appearing to be inhabited, like a zombie. What a farce... That's Nawal's Palestine: a wretched puppet show, shadows cast on a wall, with her as the sole audience. Everything, in the house, awaits the return of people who no longer exist.

Nawal browns garlic and onion in the saucepan. She pours in some water.

"I was such a little thing, I could have been born anywhere in the world, anywhere in the universe, and I was born here in God's land. We lived by the sea."

She adds a dash of allspice.

"The sea, Faysal, can you imagine that, the sea? Our village. You also come from down there, you come from north and south, east and west, from this country pulsing, pulsing, pulsing with life through the day and through the night."

She peels some carrots and tosses them in the saucepan one by one.

"I saw them come that year. The almond trees were in bloom and my father was in his office. I heard shouts, gunshots. Mama understood immediately, she yelled at Baba, 'I told you! I told you!' and she came and picked me up and she opened a suitcase and she threw in everything she could think of. And she reassured me, 'We'll come back next week, we're going on holiday to your aunt's, OK?' and we went out through the back door."

She drops some chickpeas into the broth.

"And our trip on foot took two days, all I remember now is the land's beauty, the hills' way of turning green as the sun touched them, the nights' way of falling so quickly and sweeping us along, endless fields, God who was there, all around, along the paths and under the stars, the people we saw on the way, here and there, just like us, crying, wondering where to go next.

"Baba broke after that. In half, just like that."

Nawal, now looking witchy, drops fistfuls of cardamom in the broth.

"Mama was another story. And we were with the rest of my family living in the next village over. The rest of the village, though..."

She adds some bay leaves.

"Most were massacred that day. Not a soul, apart from me, still remembers the name of my village. But God, Faysal, how can I explain that this was the first time that I ever saw my whole country, as far as the eye can see, my whole country shaking, dancing, being born?"

She looks at the broth.

"The first time I understood that I would do absolutely anything."

She dips a spoon in the broth and brings it to my mouth.

"Tastes nice, doesn't it? The first time I understood that it would always be here in my belly, and here in my throat, and here in my nose and my ears, and that it was a blessing."

She turns down the flame.

"I could have been born on Mars or in China, and I had been born in the holiest land in the world. How, in my whole life, could I live up to that?

"And see them now. They're glancing over their shoulders like thieves; they're covering up all traces of their crime.

I almost feel sorry for them: that hopelessness, that need to lie. Here in this land of God – this land... what would it be without us? Nothing. A dead land.

"So I spent my life trying. Doing right by all that I had been given. Do you understand? I don't live in the past, Faysal, I know you think I do. I don't feel any nostalgia. I live in the future, one in which our worlds have been mended and our land has been restored to the purity of a morning pulsing with life."

The days have lost their contours, time doesn't really pass any more, the hours float away one by one. I'll often sleep the whole day. The evenings with Nawal have no shape to them. She talks about the past, about a people that's waiting, she repeats, she recreates, she regales. And I think about writing to you, I think about recasting you, reinventing you so I can tell you all this.

I was lying on the sofa and leafing through the countless photo albums. Ever-devoted Nawal brought tea and coffee and lemonade. Vodka for herself. She whined constantly about memories. I didn't know if she was hoping that I'd jot them down or if she just needed to get things off her chest. I was so desperate to disappear. To be a blank slate. As she talked, I inspected the photos. I looked at the priest and examined his face, how he's been changing, how furrows are subtly beginning to crease his brow and make him seem all the more leonine. Nawal didn't need me to listen to her. I was staring at the folds of the priest's robe to make out the body beneath. Slender and sturdy, doubtlessly. If his thick beard, with its streaks of white, was anything to go by, the rest of him had to have been likewise.

There was a photo of Ayub, no longer a child, not yet a teenager, and the priest, together on the very sofa I was lying on. They are looking straight ahead at the camera. Ayub has his hands in his lap, a well-behaved boy. The priest is smiling. I took the photo out of the album (I wasn't supposed to; Nawal had told me not to, but she was so caught up in her own story that she didn't notice).

I still have it with me. I look at it every day.

One day, I was at my desk writing a letter and you came in and sat on the bed. I could feel you behind me. I was penning a letter to the governorate. I wanted to sort out the matter of this house before leaving.

"Aren't you going to ask why I came?"

Wait, wait, just one minute. *My lawyer, Mr J... a historic residence that we would be delighted to leave to the government for...*

"Faysal?"

"Yes?" I didn't look up. I noticed, somewhat wearily, my childish writing, my clumsy Arabic.

"Why a letter?"

"I have to send them a fax."

"A fax?"

"Yes, otherwise they'll never get it. Anyway. What were you saying?"

"You know I love you."

I remember the effect those words had. I felt ashamed. I think I blushed. Here, in this house, their reverberation was indecent. I wanted to curl up and disappear. You, George, had said those words. You were just a shade, a silhouette whose contours, for just one second, cleared away the wiswis.

And now you're far away – in my mind, a speck of dust compared to the figure of Nawal.

I didn't answer, I could feel my whole body reddening, my shoulders sagging under the weight of my shame. *Please do not hesitate to speak with Mr J. for further... Given recent developments and out of concern that the house may be seized by the Judea–Samaria Armed Forces, I am writing to you...*

You looked at me. You didn't stop looking at me, I could feel your eyes on my back.

I believe it is of utmost importance to preserve, in this time of upheaval, our Palestinian heritage. Yes, yes, I believe it. Deep down. *Accordingly, it seems wise for the minister to outline the process to follow, the measures to take in order to ensure the integrity of this edifice. The palace of So-and-So,* I cross that out, let's just go with "Ibrahim", *the palace of Ibrahim T., pasha, is part of a singular Palestinian cultural heritage that now more than ever it is essential to preserve. The village of Jabalayn, abandoned for twenty years now, is a testament to the richness of Palestinian culture and society.*

You looked at me and I knew what you were thinking: that, in writing this language that was foreign to you, I was pushing you away from me.

I hunched over even more; I was burning with shame.

You stood up and you left.

Nawal was furious.

"Leaving the house to the government? A gang of good-for-nothings, brainless administrators who'd sell it to the highest bidder, to, to… oh, they'd sell this dear house off to those damn Bedouins! And either way, Bedouins or not, the settlers will move in and occupy the house. They'll keep their donkeys in the drawing room."

"What do you mean, the settlers? Of course not!"

"The – the – the Bedouins. And then the settlers will come with their gaggles of kids and there'll be donkeys, Bedouins, settlers' kids – no, absolutely not."

"No, no," I told her, "maybe the Ministry of – the Ministry of Culture will make it, I don't know, a museum?"

"The Ministry of Culture?" She was beside herself. "Sell-outs, they're sell-outs, you're going to hand the house over to sell-outs who'll sell out their heart their arse and then the house? And what do you think you're doing, writing to the governor? What's that man going to do? We'd be lucky if he even bothered to wipe his arse with your letter. Some governor, and some ministry, they can't set up a meeting, they won't put up a fight against the Judea–Samaria Armed Forces!"

I lay on the white shag carpet, watching TV at Joséphine's. The house was glowing red. Ayub spread out on the golden ottoman and watched with me. He had on a big grey tank top that bared his armpits and showed off his wiry muscles. He was regal. His collarbones were like valleys. Cliffs. To his right, Joséphine was perched in a low red chair. Her head rested on her two hands propped up on the ottoman. She watched Ayub. It was five o'clock and already dark out. The house was glowing red. It felt nice. Ayub said things I couldn't make out to Joséphine. I didn't care. I just wanted them to keep talking. I felt safe. He compared her to each flower in the garden. He said, "You're a rose, you're a tulip, you're a daisy." As a joke, probably: they chuckled at each flower name. Joséphine didn't make me think of a flower.

At home, there was a pretty painting in the Jaffa room. A young woman in a dress, turned away, in the mountains. Clearly Palestinian; I recognised the dress. Even with her back to the painter, I could tell she was beautiful. Otherwise, he wouldn't have painted her. I didn't recognise the mountains, though. They were so tall they just about poked through the clouds and touched the sky. They made an amphitheatre of sorts. Snow capped the peaks. The lady was looking around for the sea. At her feet were white flowers. A carpet stretching out to the cliff.

When he was outstretched on the ottoman like this,

his throat pale and his head practically teetering above his shoulders, Ayub looked like one of those flowers by the cliff.

Joséphine must have read my mind because she said to Ayub, "*You're* the flower." He told her that he'd be whatever she wanted so long as she'd keep him. She replied, "Then you can be a flower."

*

Sunday. Ten in the morning. At Mass. The church was in the middle of the village. It was a small white building. Nobody would have guessed from its outside how full of colour it was inside. I sat at the very back. Every Sunday it was a struggle: Jeannette insisted that I sit with them up front; I wanted to stay in the back so I could sneak out when I was bored. Ayub spoke up. I won. I looked at the ceiling and all the figures floating above me: Jesus, the saints, people I didn't know, in coral or saffron or ruby clothes or perhaps emerald green or an indefinable blue that could be azure or royal. Beautiful clothes that I would have loved to wear, that I would have loved to see Ayub, more than anyone else, wear. Ayub stood, leaning forward. He had curly hair and he would have been so handsome up there. On Sundays, he dressed up. He had on a suit. He dressed up because immediately after, he would skip the usual family lunch to go to Joséphine's. His shirt was white. I waited impatiently for Sundays. I was bored at Mass, but I watched Ayub. Ayub, followed, protected, beheld by all the gods and all the saints. Ayub handsome enough to charm a demon.

*

A knock came at the door. The house shook: I could tell danger had reached us. I recognised the Israeli accent in the Arabic words: "Open up!" I was petrified. They'd come for me. They'd come for Ayub. Joséphine opened the door slightly. But Ayub had promised that he'd be a flower.

"You're Joséphine," the soldier said.

She said, "Yes."

"You're the sister of..." I didn't hear the name.

She said, "Yes."

"Come with us."

She said, "No."

Joséphine was very calm but Ayub wasn't. He got off the ottoman and ran to yell in Arabic, in Hebrew, in English. One of the solders had Joséphine's arms behind her back and the other had shoved Ayub to the floor.

He was still shouting but I could see he was terrified.

Joséphine was calm. She said, "Leave him be." She struggled, but calmly. Another soldier – a woman – slapped her. I shrieked she shrieked Ayub with his head on the shag carpet shrieked too.

"Take him instead," said a soldier, "he counts double."

They took Ayub, in his pretty grey tank top, a flower lost in the night. I rushed to the bedroom, I got his sweater, I didn't want him to catch a chill, and I ran after them but their jeep was already far off.

*

Jeannette rushed down the hill. She was livid with rage. I lagged behind. Sometimes I hid behind a tree when she stopped to catch her breath. She kept saying, "Moron, moron, moron" and "Bitch, bitch, bitch."

She got to the bottom and Joséphine was already on the front step. Jeannette kept yelling, "Bitch, bitch, slut, stupid bitch, filthy damn bitch." I did feel a bit bad for Jeannette. She was only being so harsh because she loved her brother. Joséphine's eyes were downcast. She listened. Jeannette said things I couldn't make out, "Your sister, your good-for-nothing sister," then, "Your mother, your long-suffering mother, what did she do to deserve" – I didn't hear the word – "like you?"

That evening, I went to Joséphine's.

"What do we do? What do we *do*?"

She smiled and told me not to worry. "We'll get your dear uncle out."

"Did they take him because of you?"

She said no. I always believed Joséphine. "We'll get him out my dear. Take my hand. It's OK. Look at me. Keep thinking about Ayub."

I kept thinking about Ayub and I prayed that Joséphine really was a witch.

*

I didn't trust anyone on the higher hill so I asked Joséphine: "What did you do?"

She started crying, as if I'd pinched her hard. "I didn't do anything. You know how it is."

"No, I don't know."

"You need to always pay attention, always, OK?"

"Why are they punishing us? Who decided they could punish us?"

"Nobody, Faysal, and one day when you're all grown up you'll move away and one day you'll come back and you'll see how nice it can be."

Sometimes, not often, I said to her what I didn't dare to say on the higher hill. I told her, "I'm scared." She hugged me.

When a glass shatters on the floor, there's a half-second in which everyone, shocked, holds their breath.

I still remember, George. You didn't go unnoticed here. I laid my head on your chest. Through the window, I could see the world outside – so real, so near. Climb out, go down the hill, and I'd be back in reality.

"I'm worried about you."

When you spoke, I heard your voice from afar, as if you were speaking from another country, as if it took a long journey across oceans for your words to reach my ears.

"No, don't worry. All is well. I have to stay here for a bit to take care of this and that. A house is a real responsibility, you know."

"Don't you want to sell it?"

I heard Nawal gasp in the sitting room.

"What's that noise?"

"Nothing, nothing, don't worry. It's probably the wind. An old house like this will make all sorts of weird sounds."

"What's keeping you here?"

"I have to take care of the house and the legal formalities and..." I tried to think of logical, convincing arguments, but I couldn't find any. "The laws are different here, you know. I have to be on the premises. It'll take a month or two. I have a cousin who'll come in next week, don't worry, you can go tomorrow, I'll be back soon, I won't be alone. And I have to go through everything, you know, clean up this mess a bit, and there needs to be a home inspection, so, well, plenty of things to deal with, you can go back, yes, you really don't have to worry."

You answered, "I know," but I wasn't really listening. I wish I'd listened more carefully, had you get me out of here, how I wish I'd listened more carefully to this George who'd come for me, George who'd gone looking for me, to carry me away from this castle stuck in time that I'm lost in, but it was too late, I heard your voice from afar, I wasn't really listening to the heartbeat in your chest and you were already non-existent.

I kept on talking, "Also, your rental car, it can't be insured here, it's too dangerous, after all. It's best if you head back, I can write to you every day if you'd like, you should go," now it was Nawal talking for me, "you should go, I don't want to keep you trapped, there's nothing for you to do here, you'll lose so much time, go go go."

"Praise the Lord, praise the Lord, praise the Lord. He's gone. I was so scared he'd take you away, Faysal. So scared to return to silence. So scared that they'd come. They will come, you should be ready, they will come. You're our last chance."

Day after day, I wander through the house. Nawal and I talk at times, but she also talks to me from afar. I hear my heart pounding in my ears morning and evening. I can't leave any more and I can't bear to stay. I barely sleep, the whispers come and go all night long. I'm constantly looking for their source now. I know they come from the house, not from my head. I listen to each object, I examine each nook and cranny. Are they bursting out of those damned Dresden figurines, the Iranian tableware, are they hiding beneath the rug, are they coming from the brightly coloured earthenware basin in my bathroom? Are they stalking me from the rafters, the windows?

Nawal doesn't hear a thing. Nawal tells me about Ibrahim, Jeannette, Ayub, my mother, the others, the cold shadows of my childhood I've forgotten; a morass of adults melting together.

"What about Joséphine?" I once asked her out of nowhere.

She stopped talking. She clicked her tongue.

One evening, we sit in the garden. The setting sun scatters light over Old Jihad's restaurant and the winding paths down below. The rest of the land beyond pulses with promise. She sighs. It's her favourite moment of the day. We can hear the nightingales' song.

"What serenity," she says. "The land of God."

"I don't like this land. I never wanted to come back here."

She turns to me. "What made you think you had a choice?"

She's right: this land is like a heartache. Closure is something we hope for. It's easy to think that it's so stupid, it's just a man, it's just a strip of land, there's no point, but how can such pointless things make us ache so much? We repeat it.

Some spring days, we wake up, there's some sun on the sheets, we stretch and think, "It's a good day." The pleasantness of this waking up makes us believe that, in the night, closure entered our unguarded mind. And, now, recovery. That land is finally behind us.

But we only have to see the mirror that same evening, see someone we know on the street and stop him, crying, "You! You were with me, back then, all that time ago, weren't you?" and it all comes right back.

On other days, in the fall, in a far nicer land than this one, where deep black forests turn orange and gentle blue streams murmur lullabies, it's a wind that rises in our soul, we think, "There, that's closure."

But night brings us to this hour, this songbird, this tree, this open wound running through the land.

The night is calm. It holds its breath. What is it waiting for? In my bed, I think of Ayub and Joséphine. Ayub had delectable curls, almost so toothsome I'd have eaten them right up.

As soon as I set foot in the house, they began. So quietly that I thought at first I had some water in my ear. A subtle but distinct wiswiswis.

"Why are you here?" I once asked Nawal.

She pondered the question, then said: "With all of you gone, I suppose someone on high decided I was best suited to watch the house."

"Oh, you suppose 'someone on high' put you here?"

"Well, why not?"

"Why would anyone 'on high' care about the house?"

"It's the land of God, Faysal."

"And God is a housekeeper for Imm Ayub?"

"God is Justice."

"It's mad how hot this priest is!"

I sat on the terrace. On the white metal table, quite a few photos were spread out. I drank some lemonade, taking care not to spill any on the photos but taking pleasure, all the same, in imagining the pitcher full of a too-sweet yellow liquid tipping over in slow motion and completely, utterly ruining all these archives. I carefully studied the priest, his stance, his half-smile, his physical proximity to Ibrahim here, to Nawal there.

Behind me George was standing, peering over my shoulder to look as well. His warm breath on my shoulder. This photo, taken at Christmas, with the tree behind the three of them gleaming like lost treasure in the dark. Nawal's hand is set gently on the priest's shoulder. Ibrahim, to their left, laughs with a glass in hand.

Nawal sat, her back against the headboard. She observed Ibrahim quietly undressing. He left his trousers on the floor.

"Pick it up, Barhoum. Don't be lazy."

"Oh, don't let yourself worry so much." His smile was affectionate. "What is it?"

"I'm thinking about Ayub. His future…"

He sat on the bed. Some space between them, which he pretended to ignore as his voice grew even more affectionate. Coy.

"What future? All of this, everything I'm doing, it doesn't occur to you that it's for him? Our financial security…"

"Financial security? In a land that doesn't exist?"

"Nawal…"

"Everything we do is as good as worthless if you don't get into politics."

"And put all that at risk? Put *you* at risk?"

"You're making excuses. I'm not scared."

"Maybe you aren't, but, the children…"

"You're not scared for the children. You're scared for yourself."

He nodded.

"Your friend the priest… you ought to do as he does."

"It's easy for him to voice political opinions when the Church is protecting him."

"Still. Your children. Where do you want them to grow up?"

"They'll leave. You know as well as I do: Amman or Europe. What would they do if they stayed here?"

"Shame on you, Abu Ayub. We've stayed here, haven't we?"

"Imm Ayub, do you really want your children to stay here for the rest of their lives?"

"I want my children to know where they're from and to understand what they have to fight for."

He let out a hearty laugh. Nawal scowled.

"Oh, so we'll join the Palestine Liberation Organization, then? You'll teach Ayub to shoot a rifle?"

They sat in silence together, not looking at each other. Nawal stared at the mirror. Ibrahim rubbed an ointment on his shoulders. She thought and, before getting under the quilt, whispered: "Well, why not?"

That Nawal's old radio still works strikes me as the greatest of miracles. Every evening, she sits next to the little device, angles the antenna, and listens: "Interview with the first Jewish family to settle in the old city of Bethlehem…"

She asks, "Do you think they've cleared out the city?"

I don't know, the programme doesn't say.

Nawal was insistent that the baptism take place there. They were in the north of Jabalayn, in a cave church where several rows of pews had been installed. Its ceiling was so low that adults could not stand; most guests stayed seated, while the most fervent prayed on their knees. Nawal cradled the baby in her arms. He had huge, somewhat sad eyes. She barely recognised herself in the infant.

Ibrahim had hoped that the baptism would be in Jerusalem, in a church worthy of being called such, where he could have invited all the country's dignitaries. Nawal had stood her ground: in the nameless chapel, where no road led, out there, in the bowels of the land.

"But the guests will get lost!" Ibrahim had exclaimed in frustration.

"Let them!"

She won the argument, chiefly thanks to the priest. He had said that not only was Imm Ayub best suited to decide, but she had a point: these caves harked back to the very first Christians.

Nawal wasn't particularly fond of city churches. She liked her places of worship to be simple and, as in this case, rough stone. The priest's sepulchral voice echoed. The church was isolated and hard to reach, but even so there was a crowd – aristocrats from Jerusalem, doctors and petty bourgeoisie from the backcountry, intellectuals from Haifa and Nablus: they were all there in their finery. It was, after all, the baptism of the first son of Ibrahim T.

Nawal gazed at the child. Ayub's lashes were as long as a girl's and his rotund cheeks gave him the same coy look as his father. For a moment, she thought: the same weakness. Then, immediately, she told herself: "Like a poem. I've made a poem." Her eyes met Ayub's and her heart surged with hope. In the cave, the echoing stones overflowed with light.

Nawal gingerly adjusts the radio antenna. The presenter's voice grows more distinct. Wherever could they be broadcasting from – where in this country is left?

"Massacre in Jericho: settler raid leaves a dozen dead. The army is opening an investigation." I don't know what they mean by "army" here. There are two: the Judea–Samaria Armed Forces on one side, and the official Israeli army on the other.

A commentator starts musing that this flare-up might be a tipping point in the ongoing events and spark outright war between these two factions. "In which case, perhaps, this might be a chance for the Palestinians to..."

To what? I want to shake the radio. To what? A chance for "the Palestinians" to scram like those good-for-nothings he thinks they are?

But Nawal's ahead of me, she yells at the radio that *they're* all cowards.

"Ibtissam, hurry up! The guests are here already."

"I'm coming, Imm Ayub!"

Nawal emerged from the kitchen, fuming. She was already getting pestered by everyone there.

"Imm Ayub! Such a lovely party."

"Where did you get these pastries? They're splendid!"

"Nawal, Nawal, what would this place be without you?"

She knew to say thank you, toss off a little bon mot, smile, give a quick laugh, she knew to spend exactly one minute with each guest, to be sure to look the men right in the eye so they'd feel like they mattered (but not for too long – that would be unseemly). The caterer hadn't arrived yet and the cooks were late and Nawal was a bundle of nerves. Ibrahim was no help. Well, no, Ibrahim was helping: he was seeing to the guests. There he was, as usual, with the priest. He was pouring the man a whisky. And sipping some arak himself. Her husband was already a bit tipsy. She could tell, he started looking like a red flower, a poppy, whenever he'd had some alcohol. She would have to deal with everything herself.

She made her way across the jam-packed room to reach Ibrahim and the priest. They fell quiet as she neared.

"Well, dear Father! Is my husband confessing his sins to you?"

"Ah, Imm Ayub, I'm simply complimenting him on this lovely party the two of you are hosting."

The voice she was so used to modulating easily failed her, slipped out of her throat in harsh, hoarse cadences. She was tired, she suddenly wanted to go to sleep right there and then. She needed to put the child to bed soon. Jeannette was holding Ibrahim's hand and gawking at the priest. The man fascinated her.

"Barhoum, I think it's bedtime for Jeannette."

"Yes. Would you mind tucking her in, please?"

She took her daughter's hand as the girl whined about wanting to stay, about being old enough, and left Ibrahim and the priest to one another.

When she came back, a woman she didn't recognise was talking to the two men. What did all those girls see in the priest? Was it his low, insistent voice that had such an effect? The young woman had to be the new wife that Skander had come to pluck from here. She giggled as she drank in the priest's words.

"Abuna! Don't be silly."

"But I mean it. They're not afraid for their life, so they'll laugh at us. For them to hear us, they have to be afraid of us."

As usual, he was making a spectacle of himself with his stories of armed battle. What a hypocrite. If he wanted to take up arms, he could steer clear of her parties. Some warrior he was, obsessed with guns and quality whisky, soft beds and the huge meals she cooked. Whenever the priest came all the way to Jabalayn from his monastery in Jerusalem, he'd just stay there for days on end. He wouldn't even give them any warning. He'd down bottles and bottles of whisky, stuff himself. Really putting the "resistance" in "resistance fighter"!

"So, you're saying..." the young woman prompted with feigned bewilderment.

"Only if we're armed. Otherwise why would they bother to listen to us?"

"But that's not very Christian!"

"There's nothing more Christian. Isn't it so, Abu Ayub?"

Ibrahim stared at his glass. He clearly wanted nothing to do with this conversation. "Uh, well..." He stammered. "I do think a solid, growing economy could be a useful lever for..."

"The economy!" The priest guffawed. "Don't tell me you're serious."

"But I am."

"They don't care about your economy. They'll have us all living on bread with some meatballs on Sundays. Is that the freedom you're so keen on?"

"Well, if you're so sure that you know better than us, then why do you care what we think?"

Ibrahim was annoyed and stormed off. Nawal was delighted at this rift between the priest and Ibrahim. Maybe he might even stop inviting the man at some point. She wanted to cheer him on.

She said, warmly, to the priest: "So, Abuna, tomorrow at dawn. I'll be waiting for you in the mountains. I hope you've got a rifle for me."

"You'd certainly be the most formidable of warrior women."

"That I would be, Abuna, with the enemy before us and the sea behind us."

Nawal didn't need to be told. She preferred to avoid political conversations with Ibrahim. Those were when he was at his worst: whiny, defiant, the most disappointing sort of traitor. Practically a collaborator, she might well have thought. She didn't like seeing him be so miserly in his finances and bankrupt in his morals. Ibrahim who at any other time was a pillar of courage, a stately businessman: unstinting with money, stinting with politics.

Had she been able, Nawal actually would have taken up arms. She nearly had, a few years ago, back in '67. On the fifth day of the war, she'd woken up and decided to go to the garrison. It was time. All the radios were declaring the Arab army's victory. She could pick up a broadsword, a rifle. She could fire at the first enemy oncomer, or slit his throat. What a pleasure it would be to reclaim history through bloodletting. She told her husband: "Ibrahim, I'm leaving. I've packed my bags, the driver's waiting for me. I'm joining the army." Not a single man in her family had so much as stepped forward. They'd spent decades talking about their lost home, their dwindling possessions, their mothers' orange trees, but when the occasion presented itself, they found every reason under the sun to stay put: "It's not a real war"; "It'll be a mess"; "What do you expect from Jordanians"... Excuses, excuses. They needed to seize the moment, forge onward toward the sea. Nawal was ready to do so, with a rifle on her shoulder. Nothing would have given her greater pleasure than to open fire on those who'd trapped her in her gilded cage. She would have breathed no last sigh. Let those men weep for this kingdom they could not defend like a woman!

When she turned up at the garrison, the Jordanian soldiers were scarpering off like rabbits. She was told: "Ma'am, the war's over, go back to your husband."

Those men had gone and lost in six days flat.

"The last Palestinian family is leaving Jerusalem for Jordan: our story from the border."

Nawal told the radio to go to hell.

What a city! What a city! For the first time in her life, she felt like she was truly living. In her head, the word was in italics: "This is *living*!" She'd been to Paris, Rome, London, even Geneva and Vienna. Cities that weren't like hers, with people who weren't like her, who did things that weren't like them. Paris was red; Rome green; London blue; Geneva and Vienna gleaming like zinc countertops. For each city, she had a word. Here, though, was completely different. For the first time in her life, she was in a city, a real one, that was beyond words. With people who were like her inside and out. She could dance and laugh with these women and men who were exactly like Ibrahim and her. The delight of recognition.

To be sure, Jerusalem was also exciting. When they went there on holy days, the Saturday of Light for example, Jerusalem was aglow. The whole city blazed, an eternal flame, the very proof of the resurrection was in the firelit eyes of Jerusalem's inhabitants.

But Jerusalem made her think of... She hardly dared to think it, much less say it: it made her think of an old woman in a fit of madness, pulling on her moth-eaten wedding dress. No, actually, there weren't enough metaphors, not enough similes for Jerusalem. An old woman and a young woman. A rude man nothing like Ibrahim whose kindness sometimes fluttered like silk around her. At other times, her red-blooded puritanism came galloping back; she wished that Ibrahim weren't so kind, so tender, that he would prove himself a man able to take up arms. Equal to Jerusalem, a city that could be at once a woman past her prime, a man in his prime. Radiant, indescribable Jerusalem. If she had to describe Jerusalem, if absolutely pressed, if she had to sully the city with wretched words, then she would have said... She would have said that Jerusalem, her forest, was mouth-puckering, like the first bite of medlar, and cruel. Jerusalem was – but, really, only if pressed – like parents instilling their children with both the best of themselves and the worst. Jerusalem was a wart to be ripped out; Jerusalem was the most precious of jewels. The city of all cities: Jerusalem, the city that, whenever she set foot there, gave her no respite. Jerusalem, the city that, whenever she left, gave her no respite. Jerusalem, the city that gave no respite to the living or the dead. Wizened, dour Jerusalem, the city that was Granada a thousand times over, all Andalusia and more resplendent still.

This city was simpler. It was merry and joyful. Jerusalem had been awe-inspiring, superhuman; it could not be thought of in human emotions. Jerusalem did not laugh, did not smile; Jerusalem did not sigh nor brood; Jerusalem did not dance. Jerusalem was no glittering gift nor moveable feast. This city, however, was all these things. A feast, a gift, a city that laughed and danced and Nawal, amazed, spun and spun. Decades later, she would tell me, with a sniff: "Beirut was pornographic."

But at the time, yes, it was her pole star, all her desires embodied. There she was, in a city that reeled, rocked, re-emerged abruptly, danced, in the arms of a handsome, gentle man, her husband, and she the young wife. If the word "honeymoon" had a literal meaning, this was it, in this city like honey, a velvet carpet unrolled at her feet and her husband a prince among princes. So accustomed was he to pleasure: his delectation when he ate, his laughter when he danced, her prince who couldn't behave and dragged her along into a world where nobody behaved. It shocked her at times to abandon herself to pleasure, but there was no denying its charm. When the sun set on Beirut, a city that gave her the respite Jerusalem never had, Nawal thought that she could have done worse. And when the moon rose over Beirut, every night for two weeks, her spine thrilled with electric excitement. This, she thought, is what we could have been. From hotel to hotel, from feast to feast, carefreeness to carefreeness, Nawal forgot – just for one second, but what a second! – the unbearable weight of Jerusalem on her shoulders.

At times, she really did love the boy who'd been chosen as her husband. Back there, because her husband's father's first name would be passed on to their eldest son, they would one day be called Abu Ayub and Imm Ayub. But here, they would always be Ibrahim and Nawal.

"Six dead in Sebastia in a clash with the Judea–Samaria Armed Forces."

I'd been to Sebastia many times when I was little. A tiny village high in the hills. Salome was said to have danced there for the head of John the Baptist and, from there, from tiny Sebastia (which at the time was sprawling Sebastia, the Roman ruins attesting to a vast city), the head had rolled to Damascus. All the way from there to Damascus!

Nawal gets up, says, "Well, if they've reached Sebastia, an hour away..." She opens a wardrobe door: "Look, don't forget there are a few jerrycans here."

Roland, Skander, Maurice, Ghali, and Ibrahim were sitting comfortably in the Jaffa room. They'd eaten well. Each man lovingly held a glass of whisky, a blissful smile on his lips. They looked with heavy-lidded eyes at the liquid as if at a crystal ball.

"Men," Nawal would say, "have a way of showing their bodies' contentment that just rubs me the wrong way."

Maurice let out a loud sigh to fill the space. Skander declared, a bit too loudly, "God is great!" to show that he was happy and well fed. Ghali stretched out his legs a bit ostentatiously. Under the chandelier's glow, they looked like huge ruddy dolls.

Roland regaled them with his latest venture in Paris: he and his brothers had bought a hotel in the ninth arrondissement, "by the Folies Bergère!" A name that made the others shiver a frisson of pleasure and Skander, who missed Europe, groan. Since his move to Jamaica, where he'd reportedly amassed a fortune that was the stuff of legend – it was said that the Jamaican sun rose and set with Skander – he hadn't returned to this corner of the world often. He did miss Palestine, but, more than that, he said with a tremor in his voice, European culture.

Maurice told him to consider himself lucky. After his London restaurant had gone under, he'd opened a shoe factory in Amman: "It's simple, my dear Skander, very simple:

the rich and the poor all need shoes. Heaps of shoes. As many shoes as there are men, women, and children on Earth! I'll never be wanting for customers."

Nawal was well aware of her hypocrisy – how was she any better than them? – but she couldn't hold back from saying, that night, "My Barhoum, our friends are all sell-outs."

A Judea–Samaria Armed Forces spokesperson announces that the whole south of the West Bank is now annexed. He names the cities and villages, in Hebrew, and Nawal corrects him out loud. "Beitar," he states; "Battir," she retorts.

"Why do you even bother?" I ask.

"To teach you."

"And when will that infernal priest go back home?" Yes, infernal, that was the word. She knew it, she could see it: he was diabolical. That baleful flame in his eyes, his wolf-like smile, no surprise, then, that he should thrill children. He could just go home, he ought to have a luxurious cell in his monastery. After all, His Grace was soon to be named archbishop. And at his age! He had to be two or three years younger than Nawal. A shepherd? No, he was a wolf. He'd come the previous day, right before lunch. Ibrahim had invited him along with Roland, Maurice, Skander, and Ghali. A fine group they made: the dolls and the priest. Nawal had made mansaf. He tore apart the lamb with his hands with an eagerness that made Nawal shudder in disgust. He used his huge paws to grab rice and bread and cheese sauce, and form a ball that he shoved in his mouth. She tried not to watch him eat. Bits of bread caught in his beard. Oddly, it was far from inelegant; he looked like a predator. While he sat at the table, through sheer force of his garb and his feline eyes, he had the group in thrall. Ibrahim, by contrast, ate the mansaf politely with a fork and spoon. Skander looked at the rice sadly, "Oh, I missed this in Kingston...", and Maurice responded that he'd rather never have mansaf again and live on a beautiful island far from Bedouins, so that was enough complaining. Ruddy-faced from drinking too much arak, the priest told Ibrahim, "How lucky you are to have such a wife." Everyone nodded and before Skander could open his mouth, Roland said, "Don't worry, Skander, we know you'd rather meet a Palestinian woman in Kingston than here."

Sullen Ibrahim didn't react and Nawal responded, "How very kind of you to say. There are women like myself all around this country. Would you like for me to find you one? I hope you'll say yes. A Bedouin woman? Her mansaf will be no doubt tastier than mine."

"God forbid, Imm Ayub! Me with a woman... I'll leave such thoughts to Ibrahim."

In the afternoon, they encouraged him to take an afternoon nap in the bedroom always reserved for him during his visits. "You can't go on the road again after mansaf," Ibrahim insisted, then, setting his hand on the priest's shoulder, "And you've had too much arak to drink." Nawal could hear in his reproach the reprimands she herself sometimes gave her husband.

A radio station: "After taking Jenin and Nablus, the Judea–Samaria Armed Forces are storming the mountains." Another: "Talluza has fallen into the Armed Forces' hands." Talluza means "almond mountain". Only half an hour away.

She'd avoided him this morning. Even for Nawal, the consummate hostess, there were moments that were too much, when it was impossible not to let the mask slip. Especially in the morning, when she hadn't pulled herself together completely yet, put up the wall in her heart that allowed her to bear the world's onslaughts. And she wasn't ashamed to say that she'd sent the maid more than once to go through his belongings. "Why shouldn't she? He's sleeping in our house, we have to know what this devil's got to hide. And, believe me, he's hiding something."

Nawal was furious and she couldn't be sure why, a blaze at her temples that she couldn't contain. She went out to walk through the garden. Picking medlars; that would settle her nerves. She wanted to expose this impostor, a false man of God and a resistance fighter in name only. In the garden, she brooded. She couldn't think about anything else. She heard a noise from the greenhouse, like something falling over. It had to be from Ibrahim's study, where he liked to work. Nawal peeked in the room, worried that Ibrahim might have forgotten about a lit candle that could start a fire. She could already imagine the red velvet curtains engulfed in flames. What an idea, honestly, this study in a greenhouse...

There were indeed lit candles but the room wasn't empty and Ibrahim wasn't alone. She was sure her heart would stop. She was about to vomit. She ran into the house, rushed up the stairs. Got to the bathroom as quickly as she could. It was as if she'd fallen back into childhood and those bouts of illness: her whole body wanted to go to pieces.

There was no holding back this knot in her throat. All she could vomit up was water and she spat out saliva. She stopped, bent over the basin, and sobbed softly. After some time, she pulled herself together. She stood up, looked at herself in the mirror. She splashed water on her face. Then she went to her desk. She sat.

And Nawal did the hardest thing she would ever do in her life: she forgot what she had seen.

"The Judea–Samaria Armed Forces assure the international community that they intend to maintain the Palestinian populations within the larger cities of the West Bank."

"What is that supposed to mean?" Nawal asks the radio. "That they're going to put us in cages?"

What was this thing the priest had set on the table? The scarlet vase made her stomach turn.

"It's magnificent!" Ibrahim exclaimed. "Where did you find it?"

She eyed it discreetly. Magnificent?

The priest blushed. "From Kashmir. Look, Ibrahim, touch the vase. It's papier mâché. Incredible, isn't it?"

"Yes, yes, it's a marvel. This texture…"

The vase, all the while, was hissing. She felt a foreboding. If she could have, she would have grabbed it and thrown it to the ground. She would have stamped on it and crushed it. She would have thrown it down the well. No, it would have contaminated the water. She would have buried it in the garden.

"It's from my Kashmiri friends. Don't you like it, Imm Ayub?"

"Of course I do. Magnificent, really. These Oriental scrolls are remarkable. Thank you, you really shouldn't have. You know you're always welcome here, there's no need to bring presents. It's almost rude, you're family to us! Thank you, thank you."

The vase was demonic. It had eyes and teeth. The thing had it in for her.

"Interviews with the last Palestinian inhabitants of the Nablus governorate."

"We're not in that governorate, are we, Grandma?"

"We are, we are!" She shakes the radio: "What about us?"

"Why don't you say a prayer for us? I've never showed you the small altar to the Virgin Mary that I had built in the woods. Nawal, come with us. It's our chance to bless the altar. You know, in the local villages, the Virgin Mary is as significant as Christ."

Ibrahim was talking enthusiastically as they walked to the altar. The tall trees shielded them from the sun. Nawal looked at the pine cones strewn on the ground and inhaled the conifers' scent. She felt helpless. They would contaminate all this with a vase. The three of them now stood at the altar. Despite the sun, it was a bit chilly and Nawal had a blue shawl over her shoulders. Ibrahim cradled the vase, almost like a child at Christmas.

"I'm going to put it here, in front of the Virgin Mary, what do you two think?"

"It's a good idea. A nice place to honour your gift, my dear friend." The priest had a bright smile.

"It *is* a good idea, but aren't you worried that it'll get stolen? Or ruined in the rain?"

"No, here, let me set it further back, nobody will know it's here. Just you and me. And Nawal. I'll lay a few dried flowers here every day."

Nawal rolled her eyes. The priest muttered and sang. She thought to herself that it would take all the prayers in the world to neutralise the evil emanating from this demonic vase set in front of the Virgin Mary.

The radio isn't talking any more. All we can hear is static with occasional vague words to be deciphered. Nawal shakes the radio, to make it confess. We have no news from the outside world.

She couldn't sleep. It was impossible with the vase down there, tainting the whole house. If only she could get rid of it. But Ibrahim would be too hurt. He'd promised to come down each day to see the vase and the altar, and he would. She would have to live with it, forget about it. And forget this perverted priest who brought them cursed objects from the East. But it couldn't be that bad, she had to be going crazy, it was just a papier mâché vase. The vase floated before her eyes. Not much to see: a red thing, nothing more. A red vase.

Next to her, Ibrahim snored peacefully.

A red vase.

Radio silence. I lock myself in my room. Under the quilt, I listen to my heartbeat. Something has me quivering like prey. I press my ear to the mattress, hoping I'll hear them coming.

"Lord Jesus Christ..." Nawal shut her eyes. It was just a red vase. She focused on the prayer, the priest's low voice. "Bless this house, this earth, this hill." His voice like a sigh of love. "May the Lord bless this dwelling and those who live here." Nawal couldn't focus on the prayer or keep her eyes shut. She struggled a few seconds longer, then, resignedly, opened them. The priest had his back to her, his long raven-black cape trailing on the floor so devilishly that he might well be straight from hell. Next to her, Ibrahim, in profile, had his eyes closed. A profile that struck her as weak. She did love him, even if he had such a weakness for pleasure of any sort: comfort and caresses; gold and silk; even, apparently, prayer. She stood, her back ramrod-straight, as if the whole world rested on her shoulders. She thought of herself as bedrock threatening to collapse at any moment. For him, on the other hand, the world was a vast playground where he could drift from delight to delight. The priest's voice came from a great distance; she was in the vase's grip. She stared at the alcove, a gaping black maw that could swallow her up. The Virgin Mary seemed so small. Who'd clothed her in an orange dress? Countless objects were set or hung in this alcove: a censer, an olive branch, a huge rusty key that opened – what exactly, nobody knew. The flotsam and jetsam of time. The grasses growing here and there on the alcove's walls seemed like pretty invaders to be welcomed with open arms. She gazed into the darkness. No light entered. Was that a hole at the back? Did it lead to the other end of the world, to Japan, to Kashmir, to the hell from which the priest had emerged? All around this hole, on the side of the hill, Nawal and Ibrahim had invited their friends to leave poems, wishes, prayers, that they were free to cram into the cracks. An idea that Ibrahim had years and years ago. The couple had promised not to read them, but of course nobody would be so rash as to leave truly dark secrets there. Nawal had never given it much thought, presuming that the countless pieces of paper contained prayers for the prisoners' liberation or for Palestine. As for her, she'd never placed secrets there. Did Ibrahim, who was so fond of the Virgin Mary, murmur his secrets to her?

Nawal decided that she would return at sundown to tell the Virgin Mary a few of her secrets.

"The radio's working! Faysal, the radio's working!" Nawal appears in my room, brandishing the device with a triumphant hand. "Listen."

An impassive presenter announces that the airport and the land border were open last week to allow the Palestinian population to evacuate. With that now done, any Palestinian person in Judea and Samaria who still hadn't come and registered was now considered a public menace.

Shit.

I wrap myself tightly in my quilt.

Nawal, oddly, can barely contain her glee as she asks me: "Do you think you're the last one?"

"Some sugar, Abuna?" Nawal asked. The priest gave her a warm smile.

"Thank you, no, Nawal. You're already spoiling me with all these treats. I'll have to watch my figure!"

Nawal was hard-pressed to say whether his hands were rough-hewn like a ploughman's, or spindly like a conspirator's. He took a maamoul and tossed the whole biscuit in his mouth. If only he'd choke on the pistachios! Sometimes he called her Nawal rather than Imm Ayub and while she wasn't typically particular about that, in this case it bothered her deeply.

Whenever the priest was here, Nawal saw her husband differently. And she hated it, considering that the priest, by contrast, had never been anything but the picture of politeness with her. Whenever he was here, however, Ibrahim's coyness was impossible to ignore.

"Ibrahim, some sugar?"

"Yes, please, Nawal, thank you very much. Father, did you see that the roads to Jerusalem are closed? You won't be able to return today."

His ostentatious way of smiling: he pressed his lips together in a sympathetic frown that bordered on the hypocritical. His mother ought to have slapped that habit out of him when he was little.

"It's just that... I do have some rather urgent business to attend to in Jerusalem."

"It can wait one night," Ibrahim insisted.

She could almost hear him purring. Ibrahim was as aware as she was of the prestige that their close relationship with the priest conferred upon them and he evidently wanted to maintain it at all costs. Although, to what end...

"In any case, there's simply no way to get to the city." He glanced at his fob watch. "It's already five... There's a room for you here, as you know."

She hated that little golden trinket.

Her eyes met Ibrahim's and she saw that she would have to insist on the invitation. The words were automatic: "Yes, do stay. Tonight, I'll make stuffed vine leaves and you can tell me what you think!" She was suddenly drawn to contemplate the figurines that Ibrahim had brought from Dresden two years earlier. They were arranged on a windowsill above the priest. Behind them, the flourishing bougainvillea outside was about to snake into the house and swallow them up, statuettes and humans alike. The blithe, sordid porcelain was from another world. She would have loved to break a figurine over the priest's head. The little dancer, perhaps, which seemed too gaudy to be real, with her rustic garb and her fake smile chiselled into her face. Figurines from faraway places. They didn't correspond to anything. They had no business being here, in the Jaffa room, flaunting their innocent little pleasures as the enormous fresco of Palestine looked on wordlessly. The peasant women in traditional dresses embroidered in fiery hues, their faces gaunt from having left their village, the men in tarbooshes, bearing that thin moustache Ibrahim tried in vain to imitate, the dark-haired children, the whole procession of her country looked at her as if to say, "What are these figurines, Nawal, and what have you done in our memory?" Because she could not destroy the vase, she would settle for storing these figurines in a cabinet tomorrow.

As the priest was bringing in his suitcases, Ibrahim found Nawal in the kitchen. Night had fallen. He gave her a warm, loving kiss on the lips. "You're so patient with me and my guests. Thank you so much." That night, Nawal slept well.

In the morning, Ibrahim and the priest went to smoke a pipe in the conservatory rather than the greenhouse, which she usually forgot about when the priest wasn't here. She hadn't gone there in ages. That was Ibrahim's domain – his plants, his flowers, his office, his life. It had nothing to do with her. But when the priest came, there was no getting the images and their denial out of her head. She hadn't seen anything in the greenhouse, nothing had happened. She hadn't seen anything and had imagined everything and that was her fault: what horrible demon could live in her to make her imagine such things? But no, the demon was her. She hadn't seen anything. The idle thoughts of a good wife in her boredom. She hadn't seen anything and everything was her fault. So even when she recited "I didn't see anything, I didn't see anything", curiosity or sorrow – she was hard-pressed to say what sentiment – gnawed at her and her head felt like it would burst. She hadn't seen anything, but she had to send the maid into the priest's room. Immediately.

"Go and unpack the priest's suitcase, Ibtissam."

"But, Imm Ayub…"

"He asked me to, go and be quick, before he finishes his pipe."

Nawal made some coffee that she brought out to Ibrahim and the priest. They were talking about the imminent war, yet another one.

"It's a good thing, yes. As matters stand, the situation is untenable. And we can count on our Arab brethren," the priest said.

Nawal gave Ibrahim a sardonic smile, which he returned. It had been so long since she had felt conspiratorial with her husband.

"They can be counted on for plenty of squabbles," she said, "and a swift defeat. Some success! All we can count on is ourselves."

The priest replied: "Oh, you're really something!"

Maybe she was. She returned to the kitchen where an alarmed Ibtissam was waiting for her. She hissed in panic: "Guns! Guns! He has guns in his suitcase."

Guns. At least he was no hypocrite. He must have brought them from Lebanon. He really was committed to the cause, if he was willing to risk his life to arm our resistance fighters. A brave man. Under other circumstances, Nawal might have admired the priest. She would have helped him to distribute the guns. Lord knows she would have taken a rifle, she would have gone down the hill, she would have broken into a sprint to Jerusalem to slaughter her enemies. She'd waited years and years for a bloodbath. But it wasn't the moment.

She wished she could quiet that part of herself. To have another Nawal tell her: "No! Don't do that. Forget about your humiliation – this is for us, for the kingdom, for pitiless Jerusalem!"

Nawal shut the briefcase. She thought: "You didn't see anything. Leave it be. Better yet, Nawal, help him. You're resourceful, you're clever: help him. Help yourself. The priest and you against them? They wouldn't last a year. The country would fall apart and we'd be free. Let him, Nawal."

But it was impossible. She would have loved for the other Nawal to remind her: "Think about Ibrahim! He'd be devastated. And who knows if he isn't in on it? Isn't that why he's so determined to show the priest so much concern? They have to be scheming together," and in only a second, Nawal was rejoicing that her husband was a resistance fighter. She'd dreamed of it. This wasn't the Ibrahim who loved the watches he'd bought in Lausanne and the brocades he'd imported from Lyons. "Condemning your whole family to catastrophe for this. But, Nawal, what's this compared to decades of humiliation and oppression? Let the holy man, the hero, do his work. He's the one who should be your husband."

But Nawal couldn't shake the image that seared her eyes. Reciting "I didn't see anything and nothing happened" in her head, she told Ibtissam to go to Jerusalem the next day, as soon as the roads were open again, with a message.

The last this, the last that... Bullshit. Good Lord, the woman wants me dead! My quilt reeks, but that's actually reassuring, I'm wrapped in my stench. Maybe the whole house reeks, that'll fend them off. We'll stay here like this, me under the quilt and Nawal by her radio talking to the dead, forever, and they'll never dare come in and, one day, no, I won't die, I'll melt into my quilt and I'll be gone.

When he'd spoken, leaving the courthouse, Nawal thought he'd done so well. So well, truth be told, that her heart had leaped with each word.

It was no fault of hers. Hers, or anyone else's – he'd have been stopped at a military checkpoint, someone would have denounced him no matter what. He was too cocky; it was only a matter of time.

He'd greeted the crowd awaiting him like a lion. Nawal understood: she, too, was buoyed, she had her hand on her heart. How she wanted to shout along with him, "We want peace! Not this tyrannical peace that they've forced on us, not this peace that has us on our knees. We want peace with us holding our guns and our liberation in our hands. Our land will flourish, and flourish by our hands. Jerusalem, which is Granada a thousand times over, will regain its radiance, and Palestine, which is the world a thousand times over, will regain its splendour and, yes, *that* is peace and *that* is what we're fighting for."

Yes, they might have arrested him unjustly, and thrown him in their awful jail, but now there were ten of him, a hundred of him, a thousand of him, ten thousand of him, throughout the land. And yes, yes, she understood.

"Don't let anyone tell you that you have to lay down your guns, because they're the only way for us to be heard, and our liberation is everyone's liberation."

Now that the priest was neutralised, Nawal could let her heart swoon over him. She heard the word "justice" roll off the priest's tongue. A pause: the word lingered in the air, and the beatific crowd looked skyward. Then claps, cries, cheers.

If only Ibrahim were like him. Maybe not smuggling arms into Palestine, if he even was able to – at times Nawal dreamed that he did and hid it from her. If only she could tell him, at night before falling asleep, "Sometimes I want to stick my knife in their guts and bleed them dry," and if only he could understand.

Ibrahim, her light and her darkness, could never understand Nawal's savageness, though. It was the priest who could. Deep down, she and he were the same.

Ibrahim, sullen and gloomy, stood next to the priest. As he finished talking and while he was climbing into the car that would take him back to his cell, she heard her husband ask him, in a whisper: "How could you do that?" Then came a sound she'd never heard before: Ibrahim sobbing.

The priest looked up at Ibrahim through the car window. "And how could you ask me that?"

Ibrahim stared back, silent. "Well, then," he said and Nawal thought she could hear the quiver of a sob in his voice, "that's it for you and us." He leaned into the car to kiss the priest's hand and whispered some words in his ear.

On the way back, he didn't talk to her. Was he upset with her? Did he suspect...? Ibrahim was heartbroken. She couldn't bear it. She said, "He spoke well. All the reporters were there. It'll be the talk of the town." He looked out the window.

He didn't leave the house for a week. He slept in his study behind the greenhouse. She left him alone.

The Ibrahim she would come to know in the months and years following the priest's imprisonment, release, and banishment, was like the Ibrahim from their honeymoon. They left, for the second and last time, for Beirut, each of them alone. And there she found, along with quickness and lightness, Ibrahim, young, sturdy, gay Ibrahim.

After Ibrahim's death, many years later, she received a letter from the priest in which he expressed his condolences and shared his memory of Ibrahim. She threw it away.

Why aren't they coming? Really, maybe the house is nauseating, maybe it's rotting like a corpse and the stench is coating the walls, polluting the hill, corrupting the village, maybe our putrefaction is protecting us.

I decide to get out of bed.

"You need to understand. Your grandfather was the love of my life. I'm here because I have a role that's greater than him and greater than myself, and greater than yourself as well. You should stay here, now. You need to get yourself a woman and some children, bring the family to life again in that small way. This house needs to be inhabited again. All of you will protect it from them and our memory will be safe and sound and this beautiful hill will remain ours and I can rest in peace. It hasn't bothered me, not for a minute, to watch over it. I've been proud to do it. Someone up there chose me rather than another soul for this role, which means I have the endurance, the faith, to do so. Thanks be to the Lord."

Nawal sits at the dining table. Behind her is a silver-grey brocade embroidered with an almond tree in blossom. A makeshift, ideal land: an open, flowery sky devoid of men.

"How can I describe this. To be born here where the map ends. Well, you do know, you were born here as well. In the land of God, in the recesses of holiness, just like that. Without ever asking anything of anyone. Not on Mars, not in Australia. Here, right here." She taps the table. "Can you dream of being luckier than that? Here, right here, where the roar of the universe can be heard as clearly as waves. We are the children of God, his beloved. It beggars belief to be loved by God in his land.

"In this pulsing land of God. Yes, when we got on the road, the sky was vast and beautiful and the land we were losing right then was gentler than you could ever imagine. The night we were supposed to leave, we found our neighbour in the courtyard of our house. She was pregnant, about to give birth. They'd abandoned her there, God rest her soul. A bullet to the head, I think. And they'd ripped out her guts. Her baby was a few yards away, still connected by the cord. They must have left her there to scare us. I don't know. We were in a rush, we didn't have time to bury her. But my mother, my father, delivered her soul and her baby's to God. Her husband was sure to be dead as well.

"And each time I gave birth, I thought of her and passed along a bit of her. I tried. I eventually came back to my village with your mother, Jeannette, and Ayub. In its place was a dense forest. Young Israelis were hiking there with bulky packs and canteens. I didn't feel sad. Sure, I thought they were stupid and ignorant, but this wasn't my village and this wasn't my country any more: what was there to be sad about? Who only knows where I was born?"

"What do you mean, recesses of holiness, children of God? What God? The one who's chucked us out of this shitty land? Is that how God treats his children?"

Nawal peels an overripe peach as she begs God to forgive me. The fruit's sticky smell makes me retch.

For several days, I've had the feeling that Ayub's portrait is scolding me for something. Ibrahim's figure is high above the dining room like a soaring eagle; what does he, the coward, the one who left, have to tell me? I'm not staying here on his behalf. I'd love to take down the painting and make a bonfire of it to warm us. That way, he, Abu Ayub, the pasha, the respectable patriarch of the palace on the higher hill, would at least have done us some good.

"Aren't you mad at him? Aren't you mad at him for abandoning you, for leaving you by the wayside like that, while he's taking it easy wherever he is, in heaven? And you all by yourself with this house like a millstone around your neck? Nawal, you can't not be mad at him. It's his house, not yours. Are you actually fond of these drawing rooms? Each one more vulgar than the last! I'd be shocked if you were. Is that what you want to protect, the legacy of a little self-satisfied dandy who probably got rich through mafia rackets? Nawal, do you know what's involved in getting rich in places like Qatar? And his business dealings in El Salvador, what do you think he was up to there? Come on. Your husband was buddy-buddy with the worst pieces of shit on Earth, and he's saddled you with all these responsibilities and you're saying, 'Sure, no problem'? Do you really not want to take down this horrible portrait and rip it up? Just wait, I'll take care of stomping all over his filthy face and you, you can do whatever you like, you can kick it, tear it, spit on it, whatever you like."

I walk out, it's already night. I'm deep in the mist. In the distance, the wiswis are back, like old friends. They make their way through the darkness. On one of the hill's slopes, I count: thirteen pear trees, ten apple trees, forty fig trees. I live here, in this fair land, and on this fertile earth where I've ended up. The wiswis like a marine whisper, an oceanic caprice, bind me. I let them. I've learned not to resist. She's right; I'll stay.

In the speech of my land's people is the sea. In their syllables is a wave's crash, in their laughter its foam. Even in their coughing, their yawning, their belching, what rises from their throat is the fathomless ocean. My land that you have never known. The land you know is a peninsula, a sad strip of terrain in a flat stretch of water. Mine, between the seas, is a strait; emerging from the abyss, an arm; after what was formless and void, the word.

Ayub was back. He seemed a bit stiffer, in the drawing room, where the whole family was gathered around him with questions about where he'd been taken, what'd happened to him, what he'd been told, whether he'd been...

His answer was curt: "Four months is nothing, some guys have been disappeared for years, and even so..."

All the villagers came to see him. He was called a hero. Even though he hadn't done anything.

The day after, we went down to Joséphine's. He'd slackened a little. I stayed in the garden. Then Joséphine came out and said, "We're going to Jihad's, come with us."

I ran as fast as I could up the lower hill to get to Old Jihad's before them. I said, "My uncle the hero is coming and we're going to sit at the best table for the three of us for some tea and it'll be the table by the bay window. We're on the edge of the cliff, we'll take off." And we waited for them.

Whenever they were together, Ayub and Joséphine only ever went to Old Jihad's.

"We've missed you," he told Ayub, as if he were returning from holiday.

"I missed you even more," Ayub replied, "I was thinking of you every night, my dear."

Old Jihad let out a hearty laugh.

*

Jeannette had a painter from Jerusalem come to do the grown-ups' portraits. He did Jeannette's first. She looked even uglier. Then he painted Ayub. I sat behind the painter and I wanted to tear the canvas in half. Ayub was better-looking than that. Ayub was taller than that. I didn't want him to sketch Ayub without Joséphine: his face would stay there forever, and hers would disappear.

*

Every day the three of us went to Old Jihad's. We were like a family.

Joséphine would tease Jihad: "So when's this rocket of yours going to blast off?"

And Old Jihad would reply, with a laugh, "It'll blast off when Palestine's free."

I knew when that meant: it would blast off when apricots blossomed.

Fat Amjad and his fat wife would be there. They'd wave to Ayub; the fat wife would pinch my cheeks and say, "You're an angel, yes you are." They didn't wave to Joséphine.

Jihad would tell Joséphine, "That dress looks so good on you. You should leave this place. You could be a Hollywood star and Ayub could be your chauffeur."

Ayub would chime in that there were worse things in life than being Joséphine's chauffeur and Joséphine would reply, "It's true! You could be my husband."

*

Ayub got sick. That's what I was told at home on the higher hill. He was in great shape, though. Better than ever. Down the hill at Joséphine's, he had on a new tank top that was a bit tighter on him. Joséphine planted kisses on his collarbones, those cliffs, and giggled next to him. They were laughing harder than ever. He was cooking. I'd never seen him do that on the higher hill. He told Joséphine that he'd learned all this from his mother. Nawal was her name. He said when his mother was really, really angry with his father, she would lock herself in the kitchen. Nobody could come in except for Jeannette and him. And they watched her cook like a madwoman. So they learned all sorts of things. I stared at his collarbones and I imagined sickness, illness, flowing in him. Was he rotting on the inside?

He made malban. The thin sheet of grape paste looked like an orange galaxy: the nigella seeds were the stars and the almond slivers were so many Jihad's-rockets blasting off once apricots had blossomed. It was flaky; it was chewy. He laid it out to dry on Joséphine's front steps for five days. On the fifth day, we ate it. He'd made plenty, which was a good thing because I loved it.

"Ugh!" Joséphine said. "It's like skin."

"Oh, have you seen skin this orange before?" he asked.

She said, "Sure, look," and she unrolled some malban over her face and bare shoulders, and put some on Ayub's shoulders too, and he said, "Hey, not in front of the boy," and she stopped and smiled at me.

Joséphine was the only person in the world who smiled at me. She told Ayub, "Don't worry about him."

I tore off a bit of malban and pressed it onto my face. "Me too!"

And she said, "Look, Faysal, I'm tearing off Ayub's skin with my teeth," and she bent down and bit into the malban and brought her head back up with a roar. I burst out laughing and so did she and Ayub said, "You're such a sneaky little devil, now he'll tell everyone on the higher hill and we'll never hear the end of it," even though he knew I'd never tell, and he laughed too. I laughed with them and hoped that Joséphine hadn't read my mind that I was the one who'd wished Ayub would get sick.

One night, Jeannette told me it was Joséphine's fault. I still felt sorry for Jeannette. She liked her brother. We're cruel when we love someone. We tell lies like that. I knew it couldn't be her fault, because it was mine.

*

Ayub certainly was thinner. "He's not doing well," Jeannette said, "not at all," but I thought he looked handsome like that. With his big eyes. Every morning and every night, I tried to send up a new prayer to cancel out the old one; I explained to God, "I don't really want him to die, it was a joke, can you please undo my wish and replace it with 'Let Ayub get better'?"

Early one morning, I went to Ayub's room and lay down next to him. The prayer would work better with me by him. It was chilly, so I snuggled up to him. He was a bit sleepy and he groaned. I tickled him. It made him laugh when Joséphine did that.

"Stop it, can't you see you're bothering me?" he grumbled. Ayub was very different on the higher hill. He was like the cold shadows. Something in the air up here brainwashed them. I waited until he went to Joséphine's and then I prayed for him.

The boarding schools. Some were on mountains in countries with dreary winters; others in different countries, stood alone in endless fields, promising terribly solitary summers. In yet another country, at a boarding school amid beautiful green and blue gorges, I got called Fesses d'Ail: garlic arse.

I sleepwalked through my teens.

Then I met you and it felt like I'd been slapped awake. And while they were already starting to make us disappear back there, here, with you, I felt like my future had to be bright. It's hard to imagine rain when it's bright and sunny. I mistook my personal happiness for a promise that the world would put itself right. As the situation back there worsened, so I buried myself in happiness here. The catastrophe came as a relief. Once it hit, we could breathe. The destruction mounted and, with every new attack, every new disappearance, every new death, I became freer. When the last member of my family died, I wanted to break into song.

I didn't hold it against them. For years, I wanted to jump into the arms of every Israeli I met and say, "Thank you! Don't stop, thank you for bulldozing houses, thank you for killing children, thank you for annexing every territory, for bombing every hospital. You're just fantastic, you're just perfect! Any day now there'll be nothing left, I'll have no more guilt, no responsibility whatsoever. You're setting me free – thank you, thank you, thank you!"

The Israelis I met were always rather embarrassed about what was happening. Never too embarrassed: just enough to seem polite. Their uncles, aunts, cousins are likely all members of the Judea–Samaria Armed Forces and the Israelis I met made half-hearted apologies, over and over, to anyone listening. And the world was all too ready to hear their apologies, and accept them, and let them off the hook.

So the Israelis knew how to apologise properly and I, in turn, accepted their excuses graciously. But I wanted to tell them, "No! Stand tall and proud! Don't you back down! Treat it the way you do your country, like a badge of honour. Believe in yourselves, take pride in yourselves, you can run riot with the whole world's blessing! We're weak, you're strong. We're wretched, you're feral. You're brawny, sadistic barbarians. And that's good. That's good! Your barbarity will set me, Faysal, free from my past. Go and dig in your heels. Don't act ashamed. Shame makes you weak and pitiful. Go back there, go with your brothers, go get your guns, and go all in. And I'm pathetic enough that I'll kneel before the fascist's uniform, the fascist's boot. That's what I was born for. Go for it, go push me under your boot. You've got that gleam in your eyes, that urge to shove your boot in my face. You know you get off on my boot-licking."

I finally venture into the greenhouse. I got out of bed feeling completely, utterly reckless. As far as I can remember, it's been left to ruin, covered in weeds, creepers, all sorts of cadaverous vegetation. We used to pretend that this was a nest of snakes. Ayub told me that those slithering abominations were more scared of us than we of them, but, one time in the greenhouse, I tried to grab what I thought was an old water hose yellowed by time before realising with horror that it was a snake: its scales slid through my hands. Now, the space has more or less attained its final form. It's night outside, the plants cast shapeless shadows on the walls of broken glass. It's a monstrous display. At the back of the greenhouse is Ibrahim's study. I step over the rubble – wardrobes abandoned here over the years, empty picture frames – and enter the room. It's bare, apart from a red vase and a few folders carefully set on the floor. Flowers and weeds have sprung up; they catch at my ankles, and come up to my thighs, ready to trap me, to drag me down to hell. I open the folders, leaf through them. Papers miraculously preserved: Ibrahim's ledgers. In his cramped writing, as if he were afraid that his words might be deciphered, he'd set down everything: every sale, every purchase, every penny. I knew, somewhat vaguely, what Ibrahim's business had been. I'm aware that he travelled a great deal, that he had friends in high places everywhere. Ibrahim embodied, in the eyes of the family and the village, the best form of capitalism: a good man – what am I saying, a lord – who treated his employees well. A man of integrity; if you needed something, you could go and ask Mister T. who went to the trouble, each month, of feeding all the village poor! Oh, yes. Ibrahim's riches, all set down here, to the last penny, almost to the last grain of rice.

All these receipts, years of labour tallied up in a few folders... As I go through them, a blue sheet of onionskin airmail paper, neatly folded up, brushes my fingers, as if trying to get my attention. However did it survive this humidity? While I try to decipher it, the vase begins to vibrate. I focus on the paper. This was Ibrahim's true secret. This, here, in a few lines, is my own secret. Who did he write them for, what posterity? This, here, is our dirty laundry. Does Nawal know? Yes, she must; proper women who'll wash their hands of their husbands' crimes have always been the norm here. The vase's vibrations keep me from reading more; I slip the sheet in my pocket. The whole greenhouse trembles. I inspect the vase. It vibrates in my hands. Papier mâché, streaked with flowers that serve as red and green curlicues. I hear a whisper outside, wiswiswiswis. A whisper from childhood. I step outside to try to locate it but now it's coming from inside the room. I go back in, and the sound moves again. Wiswiswis, half-formed words, evil suggestions. Go out, go into the woods, wiswiswis, the crescent moon is already high in the sky. Out there, Old Jihad's restaurant flashes like a beacon. The indistinct whispers grow louder and louder, wiswiswis. Go into the woods and go down into the valley of spirits. An even stranger magic electrifies the valley, covers the earth. Wiswiswis the words etch themselves all around me, defacing all that surrounds me. I come back to the rear of the greenhouse. The vase is still there. Wiswiswis.

I know, I know, I need to get a grip on myself, I need to get up one morning with my mind made up. Pack my bags. Shut the door, this time behind me. Drive to the airport without looking back, take a plane. I'll tell them, "Sorry, I didn't know, I'll come and register and don't worry, I'll leave, I'll be out of here, the house is yours." I need to find a new job and smile once in a while and my head will stop always being about to burst and splatter my brain and all my thoughts across the walls of the house. I need to get some exercise, clear my head, for the endorphins, that's got to be my problem, some chemical, hormonal thing, and then I really need to take up a project, yes, something for the future, writing, making a film, a song, whatever, so I can turn this torture, this pain, into something productive and useful.

I need to put some order to my days. If only to have something to tell you about so you'll understand, so you'll listen and not get bored. I need to have energy for this, but I don't right now, I never did. I was born exhausted. I'll try to shape my head my body my days with my hands, like a lump of clay. I need to get involved with a charity or pen an op-ed about what's going on from the front lines, I'm on the front lines after all, I need to tell everyone this is how it's a matter of perspective I'll tell you this, I'll break down what you don't understand for you and I'll give you a fully explained world, a filet of sole that I've even deboned for you, so you don't choke on my distress.

The problem is, doing nothing suits me. Being nothing works for me. Nothingness befits me. It's just like me. I need to do all that but, in reality, here, in this territory of light slowly draining away, I'm snug in my cradle. How can I get out when I don't want to? It's so hard to explain this, George, that all this is actually a good thing. The best, in fact: the world is finally in my image, drained of everything. My land is like me at last. Is there anything nicer one could hope for than a land made in one's image?

What I'm trying to tell you now is that nothing has happened. I'm telling you about nothing. Maybe you'll find that boring, and you'd be right to. I wouldn't hold that against you one bit. I'm telling you about a disappearance. It's a matter of one very slow, very gentle, very tender second, the very one that I'll never have because the settler was ugly and I couldn't ask him to choke me.

I need to fight to live; yes, I need to sternly tell my grandmother's ghost: "Listen, that's enough now. Quiet, I'm going now. I'm packing up and leaving. I'm escaping. I'll go somewhere out there, where people actually exist. Listen, Grandma, this next-to-nothing, this not-yes-not-no, this sort-of–maybe that we're living in – I can't bear it any more."

But that's not true: on the contrary, this is the most bearable of lands, my land of perhaps, my land of hesitation and apricots, I think it suits me. I was made in its image. So, every morning and every evening, I sit down next to Nawal, or across from Nawal, or far from Nawal, and I listen to her, or I don't listen to her, and absolutely nothing happens. And that's how it – the disappearance – happens.

Wiswiswis. Nawal's back. I'm on my bed. I plop my head on the pillow. I can't take it any more. She sits beside me. I bury my head under the pillow and, in the total darkness that surrounds me, I breathe. Wiswiswis, just for a few seconds, my breath drowns out the whispers. Nawal talks, I only hear a fraction of what she's saying.

The little blue paper is lying on my nightstand. I've read it and reread it. Nawal takes it, carefully, unfolds it and reads it in silence.

"Well?"

She doesn't reply. She folds up the paper, sets it on the nightstand. She stares at my bedroom door, her lips pressed together.

"Do you have anything to say?"

She doesn't reply.

When I was little, Old Jihad often liked to repeat to me: "You can water a bitter almond for twenty years and it'll stay bitter." I feel like very methodically despoiling the house, Ibrahim's face. I'm overwhelmed by my conflicting feelings toward Nawal, blazing brutality and bottomless tenderness. When I was little, I learned that men's desires and emotions could make a complicated, unreadable atlas. I want to tell her, "Nawal, set yourself free from this man and this nation. Look, Nawal, look at this little blue sheet. Nawal,

Ibrahim consolidated his fortune by buying an underwear factory. Did you know that? And I bet you had no idea who his biggest client, the one that bought all his supply, was. The Israeli army. Yes, Nawal, the army. Your whole life... your whole life, this whole house that you're protecting from beyond the grave – it was by selling underwear to soldiers that he, your husband, built all this."

"Do you want me to stay here, wait here, until they kill me? Do you want me to die here?"

"What's wrong with dying?"

It's life that we so cherish when we're ready to sacrifice everything for it.

"I only truly lived two days in my life. All the rest were life-less days during which I was elsewhere, laid low. But two days were razor-edged, sharp as kitchen knives. The first was in Beirut with Ibrahim. The second, here, when I was set free. It's selfish, but I can't help it. That day... It was in 1982, that May. I got up at six as usual and I immediately knew it wouldn't be a lifeless day. I was feral. My mouth and my teeth were crying out, a savage desire to bite into flesh. I'd have sunk my teeth into the maid, her beautiful thick skin, had I not found a worthier target. '82... I was well past my prime then, not like you see me now. I was stuck in the physical state in which I was wounded. I just know that was my punishment: to be stuck in the body of my pain. '82, decrepit. And Beirut, my one bright light, back there, in flames. Ibrahim had been dead for two years. Every night for two years, I wrote to him in a big book. I told him about my day. 'My dear Ibrahim, today is 23 September 1981.' I told him about the children. I told him at length about the priest. Our shared ghost, the missing man. And then... I don't remember. About Beirut, Beirut, which remained an abstraction. I hate this land, it repulses me. I was stuck here, trapped here like a rabbit, crushed by these stones that I hate, forcing down these flavours of lemon and mint, this spring past its prime, this summer cut short. You can't imagine, Faysal, how painful these twists and turns and hurdles were for me. I was stuck in my beloved's house. But, that day, I felt all-powerful. I called my lawyer in Amman. I made sure my will was in order. I didn't want one of Ibrahim's sisters or one of their nasty sons to find a way to lay hands on this house. Abu Ayub's house. My house. They would have. I hung up. My blood was boiling. I walked out into the garden. I walked slowly and surely to the almond tree. I picked two dozen almonds. I came back in. The children were at school. Jeannette in Jerusalem. I went into the kitchen. I got the wooden mortar and pestle. And I ground for ages and ages. Slowly, surely. I made a sage tisane. I remember putting on a dress that an Assyrian seamstress had offered me; her little shop was at the entrance to Taybeh. I poured the powder into the tea. Her name was Norma. Because she was a redhead, and so she wouldn't be confused with Norma the blonde, we called her Norma the Red. A name like a shock of fiery hair at the entrance to limestone-white Taybeh. I went to lie down in our bed and I drank it.

"I wonder whether, the next day, some good soul, some busybody, went to Norma the Red's shop early in the morning. Her workshop would have already been full of smoke – Norma smoked like a chimney when she was working, but only then – so much that it wouldn't have been easy for the good soul, the busybody, to make Norma out in the fug. After showing Norma where she wanted her trousers hemmed, did she pause and did that good soul, the busybody, unable to hold her tongue, then whisper, 'Have you heard? Imm

Ayub...'? And did Norma the Red's green eyes look up from her work, her cigarette dangling from her lips, and did she ask, 'Huh? Imm Ayub?' and did the good soul, the busybody, say, 'Someone ought to have told you, Norma, Imm Ayub, she... well, they're claiming she had a heart attack. Rest in peace, everyone knows she killed herself'? And did Norma the Red politely reply, 'That's a shame,' then pray, likewise, for me to rest in peace? Did the good soul, the busybody, in her dissatisfaction, see fit to clarify: 'And that's not the worst of it! I heard she was wearing the black dress you made for her'?

"Well, I know Norma the Red came to the vigil. She made her way discreetly into the women's section. She sat down. She politely accepted some coffee. An elegant, unpretentious hat covering up her red hair. When I saw her – I, too, was with the women – I felt regret for the first time in my life. Norma's red hair, a dream I could no longer enjoy. She'd come, she'd sat. She'd politely drunk coffee. She'd made small talk with the woman beside her, whom she knew. I was utterly fascinated by Norma the Red. She finished her coffee. She crossed herself. As she left, she saw Ayub. She offered him her condolences, saying 'A long life to you', in the most maternal yet polite tone she could muster, and she hugged him tightly. Ayub was a teenager and he let himself be embraced and Norma's hat fell to the floor and suddenly – like life unfurling its striking banner – Norma the Red's shock of hair cascaded down and Ayub seemed to be wreathed in flames. Then she was gone: Norma the

Red had climbed into the cab waiting for her, and headed back to Taybeh.

"Every year, on this fateful date, I try again but it's no use. For a few minutes, I feel set free, a haemorrhage, a heart beating wildly then stopping, like when I did this in my life. Freedom, darkness after, freedom at last. I shut my eyes. Darkness fills me. And I wake up almost immediately. Restored, unchanged, forever young.

"When I saw Norma the Red at my vigil, I felt like I was on a far shore at night and looking at a stream of will-o'-the-wisps flitting through the darkness: life going on as I stood there, stranded on its shore."

Joséphine's clothes were strewn across the floor. "Carnival at home," she said. There was a record player. I sang as loud as I could: "Lightning strikes, maybe once, maybe twice." With all the solemnity I could muster, I picked out a long black veil. "If I was a child, and the child was enough." I hoisted it high, like a bit of night above me, and I spun around with my eyes shut. That was dancing. "I still see your bright eyes." I grabbed a fur. "Wahsh!" Joséphine exclaimed and I responded by twirling around her. "Bright eyes." I was a man of the woods. The light outside was hazy.

*

"How are you Faysal. Faysal you know I'm the one who named you. I knew your mother. Quite a woman. A bit sharp like Jeannette and sweet like Ayub. Not a mix you see every day. You know Ayub and your mother are much younger than Jeannette. That means she's a bit of a second mother to them. She doesn't want her kids being taken away."

She told Ayub, in the kitchen, "The poor boy always looks scared. What are you doing to him on the higher hill?"

And I wanted to tell her, "Don't trust Ayub, up there he's mean too, he isn't the way he is here." But Ayub was sick and I loved him.

"You know," Ayub said, certain I wasn't listening even though I always was, "his aunt's convinced that his mother died because of him."

Joséphine realised I'd been listening. She tousled my hair and smiled. "He's talking about the neighbours' son. Have you seen my new flowers? Ayub hasn't noticed them. He can't get a single thing in his head, not the way you and I can! Go and pick a few, let's make him a bouquet."

*

When it was dark out, Joséphine and I went and lit the torches throughout her garden one by one. That was our nightly ritual. The tall flames were like blazing flowers.

"What did my mother look like?"

"She was very beautiful."

"Did you know her well?"

"We were in the same year. She was Ayub's age. Yes, just about. He looks like her."

Maybe Joséphine was my secret mother.

*

Ayub was at the stove. The sun was setting. Joséphine and I sat on the front steps and looked at the fields of flowers.

She hummed, "The fishies swim round and round, the wheelies turn round and round," and I told her that I was a big boy and I was too old for her nursery rhymes.

I didn't know where Joséphine had come from.

She said, "You know I have a big sister her name is Sahar."

"Where's Sahar? Is she pretty like you?"

She said, "She's very pretty, the prettiest woman in the world. She's in prison." She pointed far off. "That way."

"She's in prison in the night?"

"Yes."

"Don't you want to get her out the way you got Ayub out?"

"I can't."

"Why is she in prison? Did she do something wrong?"

"No, she did what she had to do. Look up at the crescent moon. When I miss her, I look at the crescent moon and I think about her. Every month I wait for the crescent moon. Will you think about me, Faysal, when you see the crescent moon?"

"Is Ayub going to die?" I asked Joséphine since she was the only one who'd tell me the truth. She pulled me tightly into her arms like she'd been doing often lately. The wind whistled above us and made the almond trees shake.

*

We were at Old Jihad's. He'd saved us the table by the bay window. He sat with us. He'd never done that. The whole valley down below was like an ocean and the lit-up houses were stars.

"See," I told Joséphine, "the rocket finally blasted off. Palestine's free!"

And everyone laughed.

"I brought a nice bottle of wine!" Ayub announced. In the glasses, it was a distilled flame.

They toasted. "Cheers."

"Cheers, Faysal. Here, try." Joséphine was the one saying that.

"It's disgusting," I said.

"You'll like it later."

Ayub's face got a bit red whenever he drank. He was as frail as a dandelion. I told him I wanted to live here with Joséphine and Old Jihad.

Old Jihad said, "You've forgotten about your poor aunt, you little imp."

And when they'd finished off the wine, he brought out a nice bottle of liquid as clear as water. He poured a little bit for each of them, added a few drops of water, and then ice cubes. The glasses filled with thousands of white see-through streaks.

"Have a taste," Old Jihad said, holding out his glass.

"This one is good," I informed him. "It tastes like flowers."

And the stars, down there, quivered slightly as the rocket, going at full throttle, crossed the Milky Way.

Ibrahim is the one I'm mad at. It's his fault I'm here. Why isn't he the one stuck here forever in this bad place? Or maybe he is. Are you here and just hiding, is that it? Don't be ashamed, show yourself. I'm your grandson, your spitting image and I'm a dick like you. Show your face! Come on, Grandpa, we get each other, we're two bad seeds. Let's look each other in the eye. Show your face, Abu Ayub. What are you so scared of? We're both full of horrors. Yes, he's here. Yes, he's hiding, he's ashamed. That's it. Well, show your face, Ibrahim, let me see you.

She's talking to me, she's pretending to, but all this while you're the one she's talking to. She sees you in me the way you see yourself in me. Do you want to feel any fondness for yourself? Well, you just had to wait a few generations but here I am, stuck in this house, alone, all yours. Come on, my patriarch, my forebear.

Well, my progenitor, how did you die? It's odd, among all the pictures of you, looking coy and full of yourself, I haven't found a single one showing your life after forty. Did you have delicately creased, practically hand-chiselled wrinkles? Or did you die like the others, sagging under huge skin folds, oversized nose and ears, bushy hair growing out of every single orifice? Lousy eyes, puckered lips... You the traitor, you the underwear seller. You a slimy soul like me. I did get a lot out of all that business of yours, out of those millions of pairs of underwear sold to millions of soldiers. It paid for a very comfortable life. While your wife played at taking up arms, you were selling underwear – hand-sewn! – to the army. All so your fortune and your ambitions could die with me. Brilliant, Gramps, really brilliant.

You won, I'm staying, I'm not going anywhere. Bravo good sir, bravo this whole family! Come on out, my forefather, come on out. I want to see what you look like.

"The first time Ibrahim saw the priest, even I could tell what he was feeling. I, his wife, I knew what it was like for him to see such tantalising flesh. A wild animal's flesh. All he'd known until then had been a long string of little village girls with big teeth and eyes so dark that you could lose yourself in them. And then this man, so different that he might as well be from another planet. Ibrahim was so delicate that you just wanted to put your hands all around him to keep the light from going right through him. I really do think it was about flesh. Ibrahim's had driven me crazy and it drove the priest crazy too. A fine lampshade you didn't want to damage. As if he lived in another dimension and occasionally appeared to us with great difficulty, only through total concentration. And this massive... being, the priest, that hulking, hairy thing. The very thought makes me want to retch."

Seriously, who does she think she's fooling? He didn't dare touch him? Yeah, right! I just know it. He was sniffing him out. A wild dog, drooling over him. He spent ten years of his life sniffing around for him. They didn't understand each other, they sniffed at each other, sometimes, it was just too much, the priest couldn't restrain himself, he inhaled Ibrahim, licked him, he'd have torn the man's skin off if he could have. Did they know that the one peddled underwear and the other guns? Maybe it was an enormous conspiracy, the heist of the century in Palestine – briefs and rifles. Maybe that just turned them on even more.

Ibrahim set his hand on the priest's young and surprisingly hairless chest. He exhaled, "God," an exclamation of wonder that he felt like he was using for the first time in his life, without an ounce of blasphemy. His fingers were bleeding. That morning, she'd asked him to lug the wooden crates in which she'd store the Dresden figurines; the slats had been thick with splinters. His fingers gently marked the priest's face.

The sun's heat was all the more intense through the greenhouse panes. "Wait, wait, back there." He took the priest's hand and led him through the jungle, past cacti and sagging palm trees, to the room in the back where it was cooler. The walls were padded with red cloth and the garnet curtains filtered the noontime summer light as if through stained glass. The study's accoutrements – silks, brocades, carpets, mirrors, a magnifying glass on the desk – radiated a purplish halo and the priest's tanned body was tinged deep red while his own pale skin was now ruddy. Ibrahim was reminded of his fingers splitting open a pomegranate. They spoke no words. Ibrahim stood, unmoving. The priest took his hand. His fingers slipped in between the other's and raised them to the light. He smiled with half his mouth so perfectly as to recall a wounded wolf. The man made to speak but Ibrahim shushed him. He wanted to hear the man's breath and his own and his heartbeat. He wanted to remember this moment for every single day of his life. He brought his hands beneath the priest's cape. His face was inches from the other's and he smelled, could practically taste, the meal that Nawal had cooked for them. He smelled, on the other's forehead, his sweat. The greenhouse's warm air flooded the room and set the curtains fluttering. The priest parted his lips again to speak. Ibrahim, whose hands remained flat against the priest's back, pinched him as he gave a click of the tongue; the priest let out a soft laugh. Lamb, aubergine. His neck was rosy, almost the colour of Ibrahim's tongue. He took in every detail. The priest's garments were scratchy. How ever did the man wear that all day long? The two took off their shoes in a rush. Their burst of enthusiasm made them giggle.

In no time, the rug was as soft as velvet against his bare feet, then against his knees. His body was no longer just a jumble of disjointed parts but a whole. There was a logic to it. He sank into the cloth, the garments on the floor, the sound his fob watch made as it landed with such gentleness on the rug. Light poured in and slipped away again as the curtains moved slowly, it set different colours dancing on one man's body and then the other's. A sharp smell led him this way then that again. His fingers, bleeding even more profusely, marked the priest's chest, the priest's hips, the priest's legs, the priest's feet.

The man lifted Ibrahim's arm and ran his tongue over his armpit. His thick beard, when he opened his mouth, was like a lion's. He sensed the symmetry in their beards, the resonance in their bodies, as if each man's skin thrummed to the other's vibration. He wanted to laugh or wind the other man's beard into a plait, or take his hat and dance, or run into the garden, yelling, "Ibrahim it's me it's me Ibrahim."

They lay together, surrounded by cloth and down. Even in the heat they took pleasure in covering each other, uncovering each other, hiding and showing themselves. Then the priest, holding Ibrahim by the waist, drew him close. As he pulled his face back, a thin string of saliva, like a crystal bridge, bound the one to the other.

Outside, the flowers exuded a hot, secret scent under the almond trees. Nawal watched.

Ayub didn't come down to Joséphine's any more. He was too sick. He got out of bed each day to walk in the garden, and Jeannette or one of the cold shadows held him up. His pyjamas flapped around his body. Jeannette washed and ironed them every day. That was how I knew she loved him. There was a pair of pyjamas with navy-blue bottoms and thick white stripes. There was a pair with thin white and crimson stripes. My favourite was all white and the top had prancing deer and trees and bits of green. When Ayub had that on, he was almost a wild god, and all the deer were his creatures and all the woods were his. He was the colour of a spring flower.

But I came down to Joséphine's each day. On the way, I picked almonds to bring to her. I demanded that she tell me why she didn't come up. She could clear the poison in the air. She promised me she'd come up. She asked me to tell her about Ayub. I told her about his pyjamas. But I didn't want her to be sad so to make her laugh I went into the kitchen, found the malban and put some on my face and I came back to the sitting room with a roar.

*

I wasn't allowed to go down to Joséphine's any more. Last time, I peeled the malban off my face and tore it in three and told her, "You eat that piece and I'll eat this piece and I'll give Ayub the last one and then nothing can keep us apart."

When I walked into his room, Ayub was vomiting into a pail that Jeannette had set at the foot of his bed. When he was done and Jeannette was off to empty the pail, I went over to him, put the bit of malban on his nightstand and I whispered, "It's from Joséphine." He raised his head, his mouth filthy and his brow drenched in sweat, and he gave me a baleful glare.

*

I sat on the edge of the cliff, with my feet dangling in the void. I stared straight ahead at Old Jihad's restaurant. I didn't want to look down. I didn't blink so I wouldn't have to look down. I looked down. Joséphine's house had withered. The garden looked sick.

*

I sat on a stool at Old Jihad's. I stared at my Coke. Old Jihad wiped down the counter with a sponge.

"How's that uncle of yours?"

I didn't answer.

"God alone has power," he said.

"Yes." That wasn't the right answer but I couldn't think of another one.

At a table nearby were Fat Amjad and his fat wife. "It must be the witch's doing," they said.

I stared at my Coke. They didn't know my power.

They'd be gasping for air here and now.

"She's addled his mind," declared an old guy at the counter not too far off.

They'd fall to the ground, they'd puke out their guts.

"Ah, women. What a waste," I heard Amjad, or his wife whose voice was the same, say.

They'd drool.

"Such a nice boy from such a nice family."

And I'd watch them writhe in pain.

The old fogey lit a cigarette. "Say, aren't they all" – he waved his hand dismissively – "over there?"

I'd watch them all die a slow death.

Old Jihad's mouth was a thin line. He wiped down his counter forcefully as if he meant to wipe them all out as well. "Have some respect. Talking about a sick man and that poor woman like that…"

I could wish death on them all. But for now, I stared at my Coke. They didn't know my power.

*

Ayub told me we were playing a game. I'd stand watch. Joséphine came up the hill. She sat on the bench under the bougainvillea. It was so tall that it hid her completely. Ayub came out and sat beside her. There was some colour in his cheeks. He'd been out of bed since this morning. He showered on his own. He'd put on his Sunday best, which he hadn't worn in ages. The clothes hung off him.

The bougainvillea looked like a house and they were in it. Joséphine murmured things and Ayub chuckled. His laughter came easily. I sat at the door to the garden. If someone came, I'd run and warn them. And Joséphine would slip away discreetly. I could make out Ayub and Joséphine from behind. She had her head on his shoulder. I heard a sound from Ayub's mouth, like a snort.

Jeannette had hair rollers in. I heard her walking in her slippers. I ran to warn them. Joséphine flew off and I sat down by Ayub.

He set his hand on my leg and said, "You're a very brave boy. Go and see Joséphine every day, OK?"

*

Ayub called me into his room.

He said, "Go down to Joséphine's and give her this note. Don't let anyone see you. Don't stay for long." I didn't want to go down to the withered house, but I went.

The garden looked sick. Joséphine seemed happy to see me. I gave her the note. She read it in front of me, then thanked me. She kissed me on the forehead. She told me, "Take care of your uncle." She added, "Come see me again soon."

I knew she wasn't telling me the whole truth.

In the darkness, Nawal moves like a flicker. Sometimes she's a glimmering, harmless little ghost. She called out to me from the Jaffa room. That's the only room Nawal will sit in some nights. She asked me to make her a sage tisane. I bring her a cup. In her hands is a box made from olive wood with mother-of-pearl inlays on the lid and carved on the sides with unfamiliar animal shapes: strange horses, bizarre elephants, birds from distant skies. "These are," she informs me solemnly, "the family heirlooms."

Her voice is full of melancholy as she remarks that, in another life, I could have offered them to my wife. "They have no place to go now. You are their final destination. Their story ends with you. The end of the road. So I want to tell you about them."

We're in the darkness and the open box casts a glow on us. I'm keenly aware tonight of Nawal's pain and I listen attentively.

"This one he gave me in Beirut. That one, look, see, it's like a flame caught in a crystal. Isfahan. After a business trip that had left me on my own for a long, long time. Here, take these two pearl necklaces. One's fake, the other is real. Try to tell them apart."

"This one is the real one," I tell her.

She laughs, a hearty, warm laugh. I've never heard her laugh like that. "It's the other one. Listen, you never know, it might be useful. Real pearls are imperfect. That's the fake one. Now take this, rub it against your teeth. Can you feel how it's rough? See its lustre. See how the light plays on it. See how pure its gleam is. And see how the light it reflects is iridescent, unpredictable? That's the mark of a true pearl. See this pink halo. He was often away, you know. I never held that against him.

"In my eyes, these jewels were pieces of his heart. They still are. Each one is a painful memory. Look! This stone." She laughs again, this time more loudly, delightedly. "One day he just disappeared. I was mad with worry. He turned up again the next day, he was on the doorstep and I gave him a real slap. You should have seen his face! I told him, 'You're not going to waltz right in just like that. This is my house, not some hotel where you can come and go as you please.' That evening, he gave me this emerald that he'd found in a shop in the Old City. This emerald that I kept for Ayub's future wife. Then when he died and... well, I thought when you were born that it would go to you. I was there in the shadows when you were born. I've seen every child of mine in the clutches of death.

"Yes, I was there too when Ayub..." She holds the emerald between her finger and her thumb, turns it this way and that. "I was the one to find him; I watched over him every night. He didn't see me, but I took his hand, I cooled his forehead and I said, 'My son, my son, I'm here, your mother's here, everything will be OK, sleep, my son, eat, sleep, I'm here.' Sometimes he talked to me, he said, 'Mama, Mama.' I didn't sleep for a second. I told stories and I sang lullabies and he was like a baby. One night, Joséphine came in to see him. The door to the conservatory was ajar and she slipped in. It was the second time I'd seen her up close, after your birth. She was older – what a difference just a dozen years makes for men, for women... Her face was crazed; I could tell she wasn't sleeping much. She took Ayub's hand and told him, exactly like I had, 'I'm here, I'm here, sleep,' and Ayub opened his eyes and said 'Joz...' and she went a bit red and let out a soft laugh. Her complexion was mottled purple, like a glimmer of death had passed over her. This stone, an opal shard... wouldn't you say that it holds all explosions? I took his other hand and I couldn't tell which of us was the ghost, Joséphine or me. Some faint light came in through the door. Sparkles like stars were shining into the bedroom. Practically fireflies. See this stone, Faysal. It's like two flames at war with one another. Intertwined with one another. 'I'm here,' Joséphine kept saying. Then she took the glass of water on the nightstand and poured in a white powder. She held Ayub's neck upright as she made him drink it. Then she kissed him. Her voice was so shaky. 'I'm here, everything will be OK, I'm here with you.' Then all of a sudden the room was reeking of almond. I let go of Ayub's hand. I started yelling, 'Witch, witch!' and she told him, 'I'm here, everything will be OK, I'm here with you,' and I was shouting my head off: 'Witch, witch!' That jewel has a crack running through it.

"She saw me. Her look was full of shock and surprise. Our eyes met and in the half-light her face was like a devil's.

'Witch, witch!' None of you heard me, I was shouting in the house, I'd gone mad, utterly mad, every inch of me mad, I ran out of the room, 'No, no, it can't be, no, Ayub.'"

Nawal closes her eyes.

"I opened and shut the doors, slammed the windows, I sent a gust of fury through the house. She slipped into the night. None of you heard me; and neither did he. He was already dead."

Nawal opens her eyes.

"What I'd give to sleep."

"My children really were good-looking. Your mother a pain in the neck, of course. And Ayub so well behaved. While your mother was outside playing some game or other in the garden, making up a whole world to live in, Ayub was sitting inside, daydreaming with his wooden horses. He was always very serious. His skin was dark and he got teased for it. This was a house full of pale faces, some people were blondes and others brunettes, but Ayub had dark skin and black eyes. He was always rather serious. And your mother—"

"Enough of my mother this, my mother that! Ayub. Ayub had black eyes and...?"

"My little Jeannette. She was serious, too, like her brother. She came to me one time, she was ten then, and she said, 'Mama, I'm going to fight in the war.' The way I had before her. She always had her back straight like a soldier's. She should have... She'd have cast them right into the sea, I'm telling you, yes I am."

Nawal laughs; she's been laughing more and more lately.

"Ayub! Ayub, come and say hello."

Ayub was hiding in his room. If he didn't make a sound, if he didn't move an inch, they'd forget he was here. They wouldn't tell him to come to the drawing room and greet the guests.

Earlier today, before everyone had arrived, he'd slipped into the kitchen. He'd tried to taste the mushrooms his mother had been cooking with herbs. She'd said, "No, that's for tonight. You'll eat at dinner."

He'd been petrified since then. Every time people came over, he had to walk around, say hello, meet their eyes. It was torture. For now, he was hiding in his room and not moving an inch. He barely breathed. If he could just hold his breath for long enough, he might vanish into thin air and they wouldn't think to call for him.

His sister, who was only a year older, was already in the drawing room. He imagined her saying "Hello sir, hello madam", without any trouble, answering questions sweetly: "What are you studying at school and what's your favourite subject?" She was doing both their jobs. Why should he go in the drawing room, then?

Now they've called him. Now he had to come out of his room. Now his stomach was in knots but he had to head to the drawing room. The corridor was long, but not infinite. He would drag his feet. He'd noticed that if he divided time into minutes, minutes into seconds, if he concentrated on each quarter-second, then time passed more slowly, and that would push back the dreaded moment. While he was dividing time, he would also be counting each tile he walked over. He'd stop when he reached the tenth and he'd count out the sixty seconds in a minute. There was a yawning abyss in his belly.

In the drawing room, the noise was deafening. Dozens of eyes looking at him and scorching his skin. Ayub wanted to be a grown-up and have a beard to hide his face from all these looks. Don't be stupid, nobody's paying attention to you. Just your mother and your father, across that way, smiling at you and waving you over. "Hello, sir." Ayub hid behind his mother's dress. If he stayed in his own head, there wouldn't be any problem. His cheeks reddened. "Hello, madam." He reassured himself with the fact that nobody could know what he was thinking.

"Baba, I want to sleep," he finally told his father, quietly. Ibrahim was talking to a man and didn't hear him. "Baba!" He'd mustered his courage but his words came out louder than he'd realised.

The man turned to him: he looked the boy over with two eyes like a fox's. "That boy of yours has quite a voice!" he declared.

Ibrahim laughed and nodded: "Yes, yes... he gets that from his mother. Come with me, Ayub, I'll take you to your room."

"Baba?"

Fourteen-year-old Ayub, his big eyes not yet morose, looked around for his father. The man sat on the ground, in the mud, seemingly fixated on a red vase that, to Ayub, did not bode well.

"Baba, what are you doing?"

Ibrahim didn't answer. He had gathered flowers from the garden and was now plucking their petals and dropping each one in the vessel.

"It's a pretty vase," he suddenly said.

"Pretty, yes. What do you need?"

The thing repulsed him. He decided to ask about it instead.

"Where is it from?"

Ibrahim kept patiently dropping petals in the vase one by one and said – although he seemed not to be speaking to Ayub – "A dear friend gave it to me. Where is he now? It's a pretty vase, isn't it."

It wasn't a question, so Ayub didn't answer. He crouched down by his father but tried to avert his eyes: to his disgust, his father was drooling. He focused on the strange vessel and his father's trembling hands.

"This vase, my son..." He called him "my son", maybe because he was starting to come back to himself. In any case, the man seemed to recognise his son. He peered at

Ayub. The gleam was gone from his eyes. When old people's gazes were vacant, they could seem malevolent.

Nawal had come; she stood behind Ayub and scolded her husband. "I spent an hour looking for you. What are you doing there in the mud like a child? I told you not to go outside."

"You don't have to be so harsh with him, he didn't mean to." Ayub, not yet a full adult, was scared of his mother. He used to be more afraid of his father, but not any more.

"I don't have to be so harsh? Do you have any idea what it's like to deal with him at all hours?"

She really was an old woman, he thought. Old age brings bitterness. They're all bitter. Would he grow bitter, too? It has to be old age, or maybe it was this land contaminating them, this mud poisoning them.

"You know I love your father, you know it, but I'm tired. I can't always be going easy on him."

Ayub, still crouching down, looked up at her. "What is he doing?"

Nawal didn't answer. She was eyeing the vase. She looked nauseous. "Childish things."

They were talking about him like he wasn't there. Ibrahim certainly didn't hear them, didn't hear any of it. He was there, wreathed in an insipid light, not seeing them, and his murky eyes stared at the ground.

"Well, come on, I'll warm up some milk for you. Ayub, be a good boy and put the vase back." Nawal's voice might have been stern, but Ayub did notice how gingerly her hands moved as she helped her husband up; such tenderness was impossible for Ayub to fathom.

Ayub stayed crouched down. He abruptly inhaled the smell of the earth and the trees that had, until now, masked the stench of his father going to seed. The vase exuded the scent of wilted, rotting flowers and the fresher one of newly plucked petals. He took the vase and made his way to the alcove with the Virgin Mary.

As he walked, he looked all around at the land as far as he could see. The light was perfect. He set the vase in the alcove and, out of habit, crossed himself before the Virgin Mary. He got the feeling the vase was made out of some resonant material.

The trees on the hillside were bathed in a restless brightness: thirteen pear trees, ten apple trees, forty fig trees.

Ayub bolted awake. It wasn't light yet. He stayed in bed for a few more minutes, trying and trying to recapture and stitch together the bits of the dream that he'd just had, even as those bits were slipping through his fingers. He'd been in a forest. There'd been some sort of wild animal, maybe supernatural, he thought, the same kind of stupid thing that the kid kept telling him about. The boy really was a bad influence, he thought. He couldn't help but smile. Having failed to reconstruct the dream, he tried in vain to go back to sleep. He decided to get out of the house. Everyone was still asleep, except for Jeannette, who had to be in the greenhouse.

Such silence in a house so full of squawking was a particular pleasure for Ayub; he savoured the calm. On the terrace, he spent a few seconds admiring the view. He could understand why some would die for these hills. In the distance, Judea shimmered pink. He felt overcome by immense sadness: this landscape had the beauty of something not long for this world. He found it beautiful because it wouldn't be theirs for much longer. He couldn't understand the nationalistic fervour that had broken out around him. Maybe he was too soft-hearted for such considerations. Hadn't they already lost, in '48, in '67, again after that and again and again? Would they keep on losing everything down to their last breath? Would they all go like lambs to the slaughter until there wasn't a single one of them left? Only the sky in this country seemed to be utterly real. It was palpable; the clouds were full and heavy. As if the sky had more of an existence up there than they did down here. But there was still everything here, and everything was certainly real: mountains and sky and dew; flowers in valleys and, further off, the desert in bloom. There were almond trees and plains covered in poppies. There were lemon trees and orange groves and, no matter where his eyes landed, always the palpable, abundant sky, and, beyond that, beyond his ken, a time in which apricots blossomed. There was everything but the sea. Nothing seemed about to disappear.

"I have to take the boy to school," he thought, then he realised he still had two hours. A whole expansive continent of time stretching before him and that he meant to savour fully. The last fireflies disappeared in the sky.

On the lower hill, the flying saucer was bustling. This was its busiest hour: old women who couldn't sleep, souls worn down by the years, day labourers, cripples and madmen; soon schoolchildren and businessmen; later, local mothers and, in the end, drunkards. Everyone firmly convinced that it was a free day. He could make out Old Jihad through the bay window, presiding over his small populace of outcasts.

His gaze ran down the valley to her house. Wadi al-Arwah, the villagers called that place. The valley of spirits. What idiots. Joséphine was probably still asleep.

Ah, Joséphine. Ju-zi-fine. What a name! He called her Joz Hind. Coconut. Whenever they met at Old Jihad's, "Juzifine" would ask for mint tea: "No sugar, lots of mint." So he called her Ya na'-na', my mint. Over time, he bestowed her with the names of every flower, every fruit, every plant on the higher hill and the lower hill. He'd have liked to tell her, "I couldn't utter your name, as if the very beauty of your name, a shred of starry night in the mouth, tied my tongue in knots and I became an adult the day I pronounced it perfectly:

> Hail to my night
> Hail to you haunting my shadow
> Hail to my burning heart
> My bird in the night."

But Ayub didn't tell her any of that. He watched her drink her mint tea at Old Jihad's, then, later on, he joined her at the bottom of the valley, in the house of flowers that she opened outside her usual hours for him and him alone and, sometimes, for the boy.

It was ten at night. Ayub stood in the garden. With the copper candle-snuffer that Joséphine had left on the steps, he put out the torches one by one. Inside, Joséphine was writing a letter. He took his time extinguishing them. He counted the torches. The palace on the higher hill watched over them with ill will. He'd set up a bed for Faysal on the floor of the sitting room, with light-blue covers and those huge cushions that Joséphine kept stored away. Jeannette said he could sleep here tonight as well. There were thirty-eight torches. Joséphine and he had the whole night. But, first, they'd have a beer on the lit-up front steps. He sometimes felt like, even within his happiness, a wild beast was watching him. Sometimes, he felt like the animal was slowly gnawing at his guts. He was happy, even so. He had the whole night; the nights were eternal. He'd snuffed out all thirty-eight torches. Those of the nocturnal flowers waved to him as he made his way back into the house. He didn't need to sleep. The flower-house would swallow him up in another time. Joséphine was waiting for him in the bedroom.

"So, mint leaf," he said cheerfully.

"So, my little sage leaf," she replied. "Come."

"You are my night my light my day my eyes my heart my soul and my hope."

Joséphine replied, "No, it's you who are my night my light my day. You are my moon."

"You and you alone are my moon."
"You are my coconut."
"And you my jasmine."
"You are the sun."
"You the honey."
"You the honey."

It was six in the morning. A glimmer broke out at the horizon like a blaze and the sky, the abundant sky, revealed itself. There was still an hour left. An eternity.

Just off the road at the bottom of the hill, between the village and Joséphine's house, is the path to our house. Its entrance is so inconspicuous – a time-worn blue door – that only those told to look for it will even notice it. Who would imagine anything but wilderness beyond it? Just off the road, even so, clusters of flowers can be seen throughout this untamed nature. Only by going up the hill does a tamed landscape come into view. Yet another one of Ibrahim's caprices, crowned by the greenhouse near the palace. Here, nature is wholly under our control.

Yesterday, a guy, a settler, ventured as far as the palace. They're testing the house's resilience, its ability to expel them. His family must have settled in a nearby village not long ago, if not Jabalayn proper. I saw his eyes, blazing with victory, when he reached the doorstep of the house he'd thought was empty. And in that moment I knew he would be swift to alert his friends. They would all come. I told Nawal that.

Nawal's been gone for a few days. She's vanished into her new laugh. Or rather, she's slipped into my mind. Her voice quivers in my eardrums. I see the house through her eyes. I see her village from the sea. I happen in the dark of night upon a woman's ripped-open corpse and, a bit further off, stumble upon a slimy thing. I see Ibrahim for the first time not far from here, then again in Beirut. I see him after that approaching her in bed at night. His thin moustache tickles my lips. His soft kiss. Jeannette's five years old, a very serious child. Jeannette, a teenager, leans over a cradle in which two heads with brown hair sleep. The priest is in the greenhouse with Ibrahim. The almond trees are constantly beckoning: "Over here, over here."

It was raining. It was raining and Ayub was gone and without him I couldn't go to Joséphine's any more. School–home–school–home, Jeannette had told me. I couldn't go see my one friend, Joséphine. And in the prison I was trapped in – even though I hadn't done anything, that wasn't my power – I had no friends. Just adults, cold shadows who hated me. It was raining and Ayub had died the day before yesterday and Joséphine was all the way down there. Did someone at least alert her?

*

I woke up. It was night. I'd fallen asleep after lunch.

Then came the funeral. The cemetery was by the entrance to the village. I held Tante Jeannette's hand. She had on small dark glasses. They didn't know my power. There were the cold shadows, a formless mass. There was Fat Amjad and his fat wife. There was Old Jihad, he sat up front, with the mass of cold shadows. There were older people, older people, so many people. Ayub was a hero who'd been in prison.

There was a noise like someone falling to their knees on the ground, and someone yelled. Amjad? Jeannette? My heart quivered with hope: Joséphine? Everyone turned, looked at one another: "Where'd that yell come from?" The priest muttered. It wasn't Amjad, it wasn't Jeannette, and

Joséphine wasn't here. Or maybe, I thought, she was here and hiding and had a bit of malban to give me. In any case it wasn't her yelling. Jeannette, in tears, muttered: "People have no respect." Another yell. It was a woman's voice. Then more sobs. Maybe it was the wind. Maybe another funeral. Lots of people die here. Even though it was day, I saw a crescent moon in the sky.

And I came back inside, I was fed, I was told to go to my room. And I fell asleep.

I was in my bedroom and now it was night. I pressed my ear to the door. Nobody was in the hallway. They were all asleep. Or thinking about Ayub, each in their own room. It had to be late. I went out on the lawn damp with dew. I walked to the end, to the cliff. The wind ran over my face. Old Jihad's, straight ahead on the lower hill, blinked its lights sadly as if it had given up all hope of blast-off.

At the bottom of the two hills, the camellia all around Joséphine's realm was practically outlined in light. Maybe Ayub was down there. Maybe it'd been a joke, a prank they'd played on us, to get rid of Tante Jeannette and live together at last. Maybe Ayub had escaped and was down there. The lights were on, it had to be a coded message for me: "Come on, all clear, come on down, we're waiting for you, we have malban and all three of us will live here together." And the proof was that all the torches were lit.

But, no, Ayub wasn't with us any more. Tante Jeannette told me he was up there and the cold shadows told me, "Yes,

233

he lives on a cloud now and he's waiting for us, in a nice place in the sky." But Joséphine had never said anything to me about that. I needed to go see her, tell her all about the funeral, ask her if she'd been there with her bit of malban and if she'd heard someone yell. I was careful as I took the path down through the woods. I'd never done it at night, on my own. I didn't recognise the woods. The trees looked like strangers.

Through the trees, I could make out the glimmer from Joséphine's house in the distance. I had to get down there. I heard the wailing voice from the funeral. It was the wind, the same wind. Then I heard voices. I hid behind a tree. They were here. Ten of them. One had eyes of different colours. They weren't the same ones as last time but they had the same uniform on. One was sniffing around. They stopped.

"Where the hell are we?"

"Those bastards just couldn't put down a normal road here."

Because Ayub was dead, there was nothing for them to bother with at our house, so they were going for Joséphine's. I just knew it. I could feel my heart pounding in my chest. My foot came down on a tiny stone. I could give them a good scare. They'd think I was a ghost and they'd run for their lives. They couldn't follow me. I was the only one who knew all the paths through the woods. They'd get lost. They'd never find Joséphine's house. I picked up the stone and threw it as hard as I could at the helmet of the guy with eyes of different colours. And then I saw, on a rock high above them, a shape ringed by a glint of light. It looked at me and then turned to them. She was the one yelling.

He turned too and saw me and shouted, "Hey, you there!" and I started running. I needed to find Ayub. Ayub Ayub Ayub. He had to be at Joséphine's. I forgot. I hurtled down the hill. I tripped here and there. They knew the woods as well as I did. They ran faster than I did. I bobbed and weaved between the trees to throw them off. I ran really fast. I shut my eyes. I forgot them I forgot them and I wished death on them. I was almost out of the woods, I was on the edge of Joséphine's realm, I saw the torches and the flowers lining her garden.

I glanced over my shoulder as I ran, the soldier with eyes of different colours reached me, he caught me, his arm was on my throat, I couldn't breathe. He had my face on the ground. He had his hand on the back of my head and my forehead pressed in the mud and I yelled into the ground, "Ayub Joséphine Ayub Ayub Ayub."

*

And all of a sudden he let go of me and I heard them shout "esh esh esh esh", and in a flash the night lit up and they ran off and it was as if the fire were following them, shooting up in pillars all around them. Was it a firework was it Ayub? From the top of the hill I heard my name ringing out and I remembered that Ayub was gone and I couldn't go to Joséphine's any more. The soldiers had bolted. In the distance, I heard explosions. I saw the fire, the fires, there were so many of them, springing up practically everywhere, spreading every which way. They surged, they swelled, they swallowed up the trees and the shrieks and the stars. The flames screamed all around me.

*

Jeannette slapped me so hard I thought my head would go flying. I didn't know what time it was. Everyone was on their feet. Outside, the whole valley was on fire.

That was my power.

"I was sure you'd remember. I was terrified you'd come back. You'd have just glanced at me and said: 'You! It was you! It was all your fault. You, you, it's you, I recognise you, it was you, when the soldiers were climbing the hill in the drizzle and there were flashes of lightning' – there were flashes of lightning, Faysal, remember, you little fool, what in the Lord's name were you doing in the woods – 'and then it was you with the gold-hued eyes in the woods, you right by the soldiers, you who grabbed the torches, you who threw them, you who would be the end of me.'

"I saw them come before any of you. The family was in the sitting room, you were in the woods, Ayub was freshly buried in his grave. I was scared, Faysal, what had they come to do? I had no idea. I was scared for you all, I was scared for the house. What I really wanted was to frighten them all: I pulled on white clothes, put on make-up, some white powder, as fast as I could, and I came down into the woods and stood tall on a rock. They didn't see me. No, one of them did, a young blond man with eyes so angelically grey-blue that even his uniform suddenly seemed innocuous. His gaze met mine and he said, 'Let's get a move on, boys, this is creeping me out. Feels like Dracula's castle,' and they began walking faster. I followed them through the trees. They got lost. And I saw you – don't you remember? – and, you fool, you threw a stone and they saw you and they ran after you, I rushed over to you, all I wanted to do was protect you, and you were hurtling down the hill, you tripped, once, twice, they were going to catch you. And then all of a sudden, I don't know how, we were at the entrance to Wadi al-Arwah.

"I grabbed a torch and I shut my eyes and hurled it at them and it was the flowers that caught fire first, then another torch, then they started running to the hill and I was hot on their heels, torches in hand, I threw and threw, I wasn't thinking and you, where did you go then? I forgot you in the heat of the moment, every torch I threw was revenge, I ran as fast as lightning, I'd become the fire and I was setting everything in my path on fire.

"Then the blaze got the better of me, it wouldn't stop. I rushed back to Joséphine's, her house was wreathed in flames. That was the only time in all these years I left my realm. I knocked at her door, I banged on it, I screamed, she didn't hear me. I was sure you were inside.

"I spent the whole night in horror, looking for you and screaming your name but nobody answered. Where were you? I spent the whole night watching the fire swallow up every single inch of the valley and the woods; the peaks of the two hills remained intact, adrift in an ocean of fire, while down below the villagers panicked, packed their bags, and abandoned Jabalayn forever."

It's Christmas. It's funny to think, "It's Christmas." Nawal insisted on a proper dinner. She brought out the fine china we used for the occasion every year and which spent the rest of the year stowed away in a cupboard. The plates are impossibly white. She spent the day toiling away over the stove, talking, forgetting herself at times, giving orders as if a legion of phantom servants was there to help cook. I didn't dare go into the kitchen. I waited in my bed, head under pillow.

When I was little, our Christmas Eve dinners were at home. But the meals were hardly intimate affairs; they were the only time when something of Ibrahim and Nawal's majesty resurfaced. Sure, you laugh, but the buffets stretched on and on. The dining-room table measured exactly eleven yards long, yes, eleven yards, and we were convinced its legs would buckle under the weight of so much food. What I remember best is the glazed carrots and the sautéed mushrooms. The carrot chunks and mushroom slices gleaming like so many lanterns along a forest path. All the light of those evenings.

We sat down to dinner early, around six (although it was already pitch-black out), so there would be time for us and all the guests to drive in a long procession down to Bethlehem. Our guests came from every corner of Palestine and parked under the almond trees. The men often gathered on the terrace, the women inside; sometimes it was the other way around. I never knew where to go. The men's talk wasn't interesting, but Ayub was there. The women's world intrigued me more, but Jeannette was there.

We left at ten o'clock at night. I'd stuffed myself on those carrots and mushrooms, and I always got a sip of champagne. It was a real job getting all these cars on the road. Everyone was suddenly an expert and giving each other orders. It took a good hour for us all to make our way out. Last time, I was up front with Ayub. What an adventure! The road from Jabalayn to Bethlehem snaked through valleys. It was suddenly bitterly cold, and totally dark out. Our procession's headlights swept the road, lighting a shack here, a Bedouin tent there, the entrance to a rundown village after that. The unknown.

At long last we reached our destination: Bethlehem, deep in the valleys, was like a faint gleam, a chunk of glazed carrot set above the world.

Manger Square was full to bursting with people. No mere holy day but lights, the world watching us, lights, the world couldn't pretend we didn't exist, lights, lights, floodlights, a moment of shared breath, we were seen, we were seen, and then came midnight: hour of my land and my land alone, solstitial moment making it whole; interstitial moment made for me.

The miracle is that the light is in us forever.

From her mother, Jeannette had inherited a love for small underground churches. She liked grottoes. So even though we would have been expected to be praying at the Church of the Nativity, we didn't go there. Instead, we ended up in a small tucked-away church – sometimes the one in the desert, sometimes the one in the mountains, at Jeannette's whim. Those churches were often chilly enough that I huddled up to Ayub when I was tired, but I stayed awake to experience this perhaps hour, from the precise midnight hour to an hour that didn't really exist, the hour apricots blossomed.

It was Christmas. It was two in the morning. Usually, I wasn't supposed to be up at this hour. Usually, I was in bed at ten. So I felt like I was in a strange land, where time no longer worked the way it normally did. I was anything but in bed. I was in Manger Square and all around were garlands of light as if the sky had crouched down, the better for us to see the stars. It was like a ball. We were staying at the hotel with Jeannette and the cold shadows. I was in Ayub's room – it was where all the men slept, and I was a man. Once everyone was asleep, he said, "Come with me, let's go for a walk in the city." There were people everywhere and, up there, I could practically reach out and touch the stars. The night was immense. The crowd was joyful. The night and the crowd were infinite. The lights were blinding and Ayub gave me some wine to drink. We waved to people he knew. He was a different person when talking to other men. It was as if, in this surreal time, he'd started talking to them in a surreal language. He was strutting around. Even his accent changed. He suddenly started pronouncing his Qs. Like a peasant. He used words I didn't know. He wanted to charm them.

I dragged my feet. He was talking to too many men, I was getting bored. Then I saw Joséphine. I jumped into her arms. I wasn't bored any more. "Do you want some candyfloss?" she asked and I said, "Yes!" A man, clearly a magician, twirled the candyfloss like he was conjuring pink filaments with his bare hands. "When I grow up, I want to be a candyfloss man," I told Ayub, who laughed so hard he almost couldn't breathe. He was eating some corn. Joséphine led us out of the crowd into the alleys of the Old City: a route some people called Star Street. My heart was pounding wildly.

You know what we call candyfloss here? "Girls' hair." I wouldn't mind some candyfloss. It's Christmas, after all.

It's funny to think, "It's Christmas," in an empty land. I can tell, on the horizon, that the land really has become empty all of a sudden. Will we, my grandmother and I, really be the only ones left, the last ones?

Nawal calls me from the terrace. She gestures toward the horizon. She came out to pick some mint for the courgettes, and she saw them. They're closing in, this time for good. They're there, in the distance. They must be carrying torches, because it looks like a procession of demons, a long serpentine light snaking toward Jabalayn. They've come from far off. Without cars, jeeps, they don't need any of that. They're coming. They'll come. They'll arrive tonight. Would they have come later if I hadn't killed this man I've forgotten? It's the final night in Jabalayn. It's Christmas. I can feel everything, even the ground, getting lighter.

All I want is to finish talking to you, just in case. I haven't stopped telling you that Jabalayn is disappearing. It matters to me. Now that it really is going, now that disappearance is rolling like fog over the two hills, now that the village is starting to vanish completely – the rocks already seem to be flying off into the sky and I with them – some sort of melancholy seems to have lodged between my chest and my stomach. I'd have liked to stop by the cemetery. I haven't been there since I came here. Just to see Ayub. I don't know. After this, there'll be no more Ayub, no more cemetery, no more memory of him. I'll be the only repository, the only memory of Ayub and Joséphine. I'd like to be able to remember, at the very least, the candyfloss in Bethlehem. I wish I'd made

246

an inventory of Jabalayn, so it couldn't turn to mist without a trace.

I know they've won. Ultimately, in the grand scheme of things, it's not so bad. There's no shaking off Nawal now. She and I are no different. I thought I might be Ayub, I thought I might be Ibrahim, but, no, I'm Nawal. We're the same. I don't want them to have the house. They can have the grounds, but not the house. It's mine. It's me.

What should I do? I ought to have asked you before moving away, or before you left me once and for all. I should have talked to you. But I couldn't, there was a black hole there that let nothing go, that swallowed everything up. And here I am, defenceless.

What can I do? I should figure it out. I'll go find Nawal. Since the dawn of time she's been preparing for this exact moment. Yes, that's what she's doing. That's why. She knew. She summoned me here for this. All along, she's been getting me ready. The ultimate sacrifice is the one in which nobody wins. Utter pettiness. I'm ready. She saw the insurgency, when it was just starting, and she thought, "That's it, he needs to come back. He needs to be ready to destroy everything when everything has to be destroyed." She wanted to ready me for annihilation.

What did I want to confess to you, deep down? That I'd secretly lived my whole life thinking I'd burned down an entire village? That I'd knowingly killed people myself? Or that Grandpa had covertly sold underwear to soldiers, and that my whole life was built on that fortune?

None of those count for much now that they're coming.

So stupid of me – sorry dregs of my religious schooling – to want to confess things to you.

All the lights are off. As soon as they arrived, I regained my childhood instincts for the shadows. I blended into the background. I'd learned, early on, to survive by making myself invisible. I'm good at it, so good that I could go to the middle of the drawing room and do a headstand, and nobody would see.

They're inside. I'm behind a sofa in the Jaffa room. It's ridiculous. Nawal's sitting, but they won't see her.

"This is giving me the creeps," says a man I can't make out. There are two of them, or maybe three.

They're in the Jaffa room.

"You think there's someone here?" another asks.

They fumble around for a light switch. Nawal is motionless as she observes them.

I feel like each of my breaths could set off a racket, raise all hell. Then I remember that I'm invisible.

They're carrying rifles.

"No, nobody."

They're groping around.

"What a waste. They let all this go to rot," the first one says, and the other answers, "Completely irresponsible." A snicker. "Good thing we came."

From the piano, I hear someone play the first few bars of an old familiar song and a woman's voice sing. They seem not to hear it. People who aren't ghosts have appeared all around and the drawing room is bathed in light. The two or three settlers are rummaging through the room's nooks and crannies. Nawal's still sitting on the sofa, and Nawal's over there dancing with Ibrahim around the settlers. It's Christmas. The garlands gleam, a rainbow of flames. Nawal seated, Nawal dancing, and the settlers, and Ibrahim's face. He's full of grace, she's less so. But her self-assurance and the sureness of her movements steady her. The music all around them. He holds her by the waist and twirls her to then fro. She lets him. It's Christmas, after all. At one point, she slips up, she falls in his arms, and she bursts out laughing. Nawal and Ibrahim dance around the settlers. The curtains flutter. The drawing-room chairs are gilded and the wall hangings shine as if the light were bouncing off them.

Then suddenly the music is gone, along with Nawal and Ibrahim too, and the fir.

They've found a light switch.

"All good," one of the shades announces. "I think we can call in the others."

I don't want to move again.

"Faysal?" Nawal's calling me, calling me, begging me: "Look at me, please."

I'm paralysed. I can't bear it any more. I can't bear myself any more. I can't bear this house any more.

"Please, you have to end it all."

It's me or it's Nawal talking, neither she nor I can bear this house any more.

"The day I... well, you know, that day... There was a vase." She wants the vase. "That demonic vase. Red as blood."

The mention of the vase gets my body moving. Crouched so the invaders don't see me, I make my way out of the drawing room and rush into the greenhouse, deep in darkness. The plants really have overrun the space, made the structure cave in. I'm aware that I'm intruding in a kingdom where I have no business being. The branches are like snakes watching me with yellow eyes.

There it is. The vase shudders and the whispers wiswiswis turn into shrieks, sharp cries that momentarily keep me from moving. But I manage to grab it. It feels like human skin.

As I emerge from the greenhouse, a gale-force wind rises.

No, it's just my imagination.

Nawal's waiting for me in the drawing room. Out of the vase come all sorts of screams, cries, groans, and, loudest of all, the whispers, wiswiswis.

I shout above the din: "Are you ready?"

"Yes, I'm ready."

The voices suddenly go quiet. The wind goes quiet. The whole house goes quiet. The settlers, bewildered, freeze.

Nawal stands, facing me.

"What are you waiting for?"

Can I be sure you really did come, George? Can I be sure I'm sending this babbling, this endless stream of beginnings, to you? Can I be sure I'm sending this ridiculous heap of lies to you?

I suppose I should tell the end. I suppose I should, as some time still remains. I may be fading like fog, but some time, just enough, still remains.

When he came, the first time, I pounced on him, all his light made my heart burst. Faysal, my darling, come back home at last; come to help his grandmother at last. I could scarcely believe my eyes. It seemed like a mirage, as if I were the only real thing.

He came that afternoon; he had heeded my call, my little joke. As if there had been an actual Tante Rita! And he was handsome, too. So handsome – a bit of Ayub, a bit of Ibrahim, a bit of me. So handsome and so Palestinian, and I thought, "How can our end be near when we have children like him?" He was a bit peculiar, yes, a bit beside himself. But what did that matter? He was here, handsome and Palestinian, and it brought such pride to my heart, such relief, and the house's stones cracked apart with light. What hope he'd brought me. What hope he brings me this very moment. If we must be cockroaches, then so we shall be: innumerable, ineradicable. We'll slip into the gaps and crevices of their lives, always waiting, and they'll always know, deep down, that we're here. If not him, if not me, then so many millions of others. So many cockroaches crammed together inside the cracked walls. What hope, what relief, that he should come, even if now...

"Quick, Nawal." He grabs the vase and rushes alongside me into the Jaffa room. They're laughing and singing; I think they're actually dancing. The shades surround us. Have they come for a picnic? At this hour, in this weather?

A gunshot blows apart the terrace door. They are in the sitting room, knocking over furniture. I can hear things shattering.

In the middle, in the heart of the woods that I am, is a stand of narcissus.

The voices of men and women shriek, "Over here!" and "Over there!" Children try to outdo each other: "Bet a thousand shekels you can't throw a brick through the window!"

And a brick shatters one of the glass panes. It comes within a hair's breadth of my head. In my woods.

"This house is creepy."

"You think it's their ghosts?"

"Pfft! I'll shoot every ghost dead with this AK."

"What a filthy house."

I can hear the children run all around. "Be careful!" a voice orders them.

Oh Protector. Faysal, do something. How many of them are here? Ten? Fifteen?

A woman says: "Let's see the kitchen."

"What's this disgusting stuff?"

"Ugh, it's goopy. Is it food?"

Faysal, you must scare them away. I can open the windows, slam the doors. Let's scare them to death.

They make lots of noise to reassure themselves.

But Faysal refuses to let me leave the drawing room. He has a jerrycan.

There's nothing we can do, if they decide to take the house, they'll take it. And they've decided. At least... at least... They are in the adjoining rooms, closing in on us, plundering and pillaging this house.

Faysal whispers: "They can die."

"Look around, there have to be jewels somewhere." A woman tells her child, calmly: "See, they abandon their houses just like that and we come to save them. We come to bring them back to life."

Faysal intones: "This woman will suffocate and collapse on her child who will suffocate too. In each room they'll all fall on their backs and they'll beg their God to save them but they'll keep suffocating. They'll scream in pain and their torment will last the whole night. And tomorrow morning, I'll have work to do. Bodies to bury." He looks around at the heavy curtains, the rugs, the endless wardrobes, the trees around the house. He douses it all. Not a shred of rug or bit of curtain goes unbaptised. Not a single object, apart from the vase.

"All right, Nawal. Let's do what we know how to do best."

I stand by the drawing-room door to the backyard and, further off, the greenhouse. He hands me a box of matches.

"All yours."

A second fire. The fire sings. Iridescent, pearlescent. The garden catches fire first, then the house. This is the fate that has always awaited it. This is our paltry rebellion.

Joséphine's plain has burned to ashes. The peak of the hill blazes in the night like a torch. Jabalayn is still in flames, flickering with a thousand colours.

He holds the vase under his arm and I stand at his side.

"Here?"

"No..."

"The cemetery?"

Some rubble remains where Joséphine's house, a cathedral of a bygone era, once stood. I kneel to gather a handful of earth that I pour into the vase. In the dark of night, like thieves, we head for the cemetery.

The settlers are everywhere in the town, jubilant.

We sneak down alleys in the shadow of their bonfires.

They fire bullets into the air and sing and dance. "Ours, ours, ours."

We reach the cemetery on the edge of the town. How many times I've made my way down the terraces of this place. All of us have been laid to rest here.

"Here. That's perfect. Next to them."

By Ayub's headstone, I pour out the earth that I gathered at Joséphine's.

"Are you ready this time?" he asks me.

"Yes."

He smiles. "See you soon, Imm Ayub."

And he cracks the vase which shatters, thousands of voices escaping in newfound freedom.

And now he sits down, leaning against Ayub's stone, not far from Ibrahim's and mine, and now my heart swells at the sight of all three together at last. And now he presses his cheek to the stone. And now he stays put, against the headstone, and now he waits for them to come. And now I tell him, "They'll come very, very soon." And now I smile at him, and now he cannot see me any more, and now I begin to disperse. And now I lean over him, as I did for his mother and for Ayub, and now I stroke his cheek and now we simply wait, wait for them.

When he came, the first time, I went out on the terrace and looked out at the almond trees and, further off, I could make out the sea from which came a curious music; and I would have loved to instil in him this thing he'd never known.

I have not gone. I have looked away, I have stopped listening. I have been thinking of the woman I left disembowelled a thousand years ago back there, far off, in a land that no longer exists.

Repose is a beautiful, richly deserved thing.

I have let them do as they please. I may have stopped listening but even so I hear, "There's one here, quick, quick," I hear, "Son of a bitch," I hear a muffled cry like the cry let out by sacrificial sheep as their throats are slit for the Feast of al-Khader.

I have not turned; I have not looked back. I have come back here where I now wait to disappear.

Peace.

Foundry Editions
40 Randolph Street
London NW1 0SR
United Kingdom

ISBN 978-1-0686934-0-3

Series cover design by Murmurs Design
Designed and typeset in LfA Aluminia by Tetragon, London
Printed and bound by TJ Books

foundryeditions.co.uk

This book has been selected to receive financial assistance from English PEN's PEN Translates programme, supported by Arts Council England. English PEN exists to promote literature and our understanding of it, to uphold writers' freedoms around the world, to campaign against the persecution and imprisonment of writers for stating their views, and to promotethe friendly co-operation of writers and the free exchange of ideas. www.englishpen.org

EU GPSR authorised representative: Logos Europe, 9 rue Nicolas Poussin, 17000 La Rochelle, France; contact@logoseurope.eu.

Supported using public funding by
ARTS COUNCIL ENGLAND

ENGLISH PEN

CNL CENTRE NATIONAL DU LIVRE

ESTHER GARCÍA LLOVET

Spanish Beauty

Translation by Richard Village

SPAIN

Michela McKay is on a mission. The hardest, shadiest officer in the Spanish National Police, Benidorm, will stop at nothing to get her hands on Reggie Kray's iconic Dunhill lighter. Up against an unforgettable cast of gangsters, chancers, low-lifes and a compulsory absent father, this punk picaresque heroine takes us beyond the sunburn and all-day fry-ups on a high-octane ride through the underbelly of the infamous Spanish resort.

With a turn of phrase that always slays, an eye for detail that is as forensic as it is cinematic, a sense of humour as dry as a glass of fino, and a wilful desire to break conventional genres, cult author Esther García Llovet's love letter to the pearl of the Costa Blanca feels like the best of Almodóvar in surreal, novel form.

ANNA PAZOS
Killing the Nerve

Translation by Laura McGloughlin and Charlotte Coombe

SPAIN/CATALONIA

Not so much autofiction as autojournalism, *Killing the Nerve* dissects the end of youth and the beginning of adulthood for the global nomad generation. Fleeing the "Mediterranean mediocrity" of bourgeois Barcelona life, Anna Pazos's story hurtles us from wasted Erasmus days in Thessaloniki, through a period in Jerusalem and a voyage across the Atlantic with an unsuitable lover, to post-MeToo New York.

When she is forced back to Barcelona with the pandemic, she turns her super-cool, scalpel-like eye and super-intelligent, incisive language on her family within the context of Catalan society, especially the independentist movement, and on her place in that world.

This stunning debut has been a hit at home. It was longlisted for the Premi Finestres 2023 and voted best Catalan Book of the Year by "Babelia", *El País'* prestigious cultural supplement.

CÉCILE TLILI

Just a Little Dinner

Translation by Katherine Gregor

FRANCE

In a tired, hot Paris at the end of August, two couples, who'd rather still be by the sea, meet for dinner in one of their apartments. Étienne, the host, needs something from Johar in order to save his career, but Johar has her own future to worry about. Her husband Remi is finding it difficult to keep his own well-guarded secret and Claudia, Étienne's partner, is stuck, facing the reality of her life and relationship, cooking curry in the sweltering kitchen.

With delicious detail and a perfectly pitched plot, Cécile Tlili gives an incisive glimpse behind the shutters of the 7th arrondissement. Fractured relationships, bad behaviour and pure desperation are laid bare in this very contemporary Parisian tale, as what starts as just a little dinner ends up having monumental consequences for everyone.

The book was shortlisted for the 2024 Prix Goncourt du Premier Roman and won the 2023 Prix Littéraire Gisèle Halimi for women's writing.

CHIARA VALERIO

The Little I Knew

Translation by Ailsa Wood

ITALY

In Scauri, an end of the line seaside resort forty miles or so from Rome, Vittoria, whose arrival in the town thirty years earlier was shrouded in mystery, dies in her bath. Whilst most of the townsfolk meet the event with sad but respectful southern Italian silence, Lea, the town's lawyer, starts to investigate. Who was Vittoria? What was her secret? Why did she come to Scauri? And was her relationship with Lea all that it seemed?

In this unforgettable portrait of a small town and the women who live there, reverberations from the past catch up with the silence of the present and everything – passions, emotions and relationships – changes for ever.

A huge bestseller in Italy, *The Little I Knew* was short-listed for the 2024 Premio Strega.